HEIDI

✣ DERRYDALE ✣ CHILDREN'S ✣ LIBRARY ✣

Heidi

JOHANNA SPYRI

Derrydale

Heidi was first published in Switzerland in 1880.

This edition published by **Derrydale Books**
Distributed by Random House Value Publishing, Inc.
40 Engelhard Avenue
Avenel, New Jersey 07001

Design and arrangement © 1994 Parragon Book Service Ltd.

ISBN 0-517-14149-3

Printed in Great Britain

CHAPTER 1

Up to the Alm-Uncle

From the old and pleasantly situated town of Mayenfeld a path leads through green, shady meadows to the foot of the mountains which look down from their majestic heights upon the valley below. As the footpath begins to slope gently upwards, the fragrance of the nearby heath, with its short grass and vigorous mountain plants, fills the air; then the way becomes more rugged and the path rises steeply towards the Alps.

One bright, sunny morning in June, a tall, sturdy-looking girl of this mountainous country climbed the narrow mountain path, leading a child by the hand. The little girl's cheeks were aglow and the bright crimson shone even through her brown, sunburnt skin. This was not surprising, for in spite

of the scorching sun the child was wrapped up as
though for protection against bitter frost. She wore
two, if not three frocks, one on top of the other,
and, in addition, a big red shawl was tied all round
her body so that her little five-year-old figure was
scarcely discernible. In her heavy, nailed mountain
shoes, she toiled laboriously up the slope. The two
figures had been climbing from the valley for about
an hour when they reached the hamlet called Dörfli
which is situated half-way up the Alm. Here they
were greeted with friendly calls from every doorway, for this was the girl's birthplace. But she
hurried on until she had reached the last of the scat-
tered little houses, and as she passed, a voice called
from the doorway, "Wait for me, Dete, if you are
going up and I will come too!"

She stood still, and the child let go of her and sat
down on the ground. "Are you tired, Heidi?" asked
the older girl.

"No, I am hot, though," answered Heidi.

"We shall soon reach the top now. If you can be
brave and walk strongly for a little longer we shall
get there in an hour," said Dete encouragingly.

The stout pleasant-looking woman who had
hailed them, came out of her house and joined

them, chattering and laughing with Dete, who was an old acquaintance.

"Where are you taking the child, Dete?" she asked. "I suppose it is your sister's child—the orphan?"

"Yes," answered Dete. "I am taking her to stay with the Alm-Uncle."

"Surely you aren't going to leave the child with *him*. You must be out of your mind, Dete! The old man is sure to turn you away, in any case!"

"He can't do that! He is her grandfather. I have looked after the child up till now, and I can tell you, Barbel, I am not going to turn down the offer of a good job on her account. From now on the grandfather will have to do his bit."

"Oh, well, if he were like other people—" replied Barbel, "but you know him as well as I do. How can he look after a child, and especially such a little one? Oh, she will never stay with him! But where are *you* going, Dete?"

"To a very good job in Frankfurt," explained Dete. "I looked after the people I am going to at the Baths last summer. They wanted me to go away with them then, but of course I could not go. Now they have asked me again you can be sure that I am not going to let the opportunity pass!"

"Well, I wouldn't like to be the child," said Barbel disapprovingly. "Nobody knows anything about the old man up there. He never speaks to anybody, and he never goes to church. If he is seen, occasionally, everyone keeps away from him and his stick. With his bushy eyebrows and terrible beard he looks a positive savage. The whole village is afraid of him and not many people would want to be alone with him."

"Still," Dete persisted, "he is the grandfather and it's up to him to look after the child."

"They say all sorts of terrible things about the old man," said Barbel, glancing keenly at her companion. "There must be something on his conscience, that he should live such an isolated life up there. You must surely have heard his history from your sister, eh, Dete?"

"Perhaps I have, but I shan't say. It would be a fine thing for me if he found out I had been talking!"

Barbel had been eager for a long time to learn something about the old man whom everybody referred to as the Alm-Uncle. She wanted to know why he seemed to hate everybody and why he lived all by himself up on the mountain. Besides, she

wondered why the villagers in Dörfli called him
Alm-Uncle. He was obviously not everyone's uncle.
Barbel was much the same as all the others though,
and referred to him by the same name.

Barbel had married and come to Dörfli quite
recently, so she was not familiar with local history.
Dete, on the other hand, had spent her child-
hood and youth in Dörfli, until she had gone into
service in the large hotel at Ragatz Baths the previous
year.

This morning Dete had come all the way from
Ragatz on this special journey with little Heidi.
Barbel was quite determined not to miss this golden
opportunity to find out as much as she could about
the strange old man. Confidentially she took Dete's
arm. "Do tell me more about him, now! You have
nothing to fear," she coaxed.

"I can't be expected to tell you much about an
old fellow who is nearly fifty years older than me.
He must be at least seventy! However, if I could be
absolutely certain that whatever I told you would be
kept completely confidential, then I dare say I could
tell you a few things I have found out about him, as
he came from Domleschg, where my mother was
born."

"Whatever do you mean, Dete?" retorted Barbel, red in the face. "I am not one of those village gossips and you can take my word that I know how to keep a secret."

"All right then, I'll tell you," said Dete, lowering her voice, "but I don't want the child to hear." She looked round to see whether Heidi were nearby and might hear what she had to say, but the little one was not in sight. Dete stopped in some consternation, and looked back. There was no sign of the child.

"Now I see her!" cried Barbel at last. "Over there!" She pointed far away from the path. "She is climbing the slopes with Peter, the goat-herd, and his goats. He can look after the child, and you will be able to go on with your story."

"She's good enough at looking after herself," said Dete, "and perhaps it's a good thing, for the old man will not be able to provide for her very well. He has nothing now but his two goats and the Alm cottage."

"Did he have more in his younger days?" asked Barbel.

"Yes, I should think he did!" replied Dete with conviction. "He was brought up on one of the finest

farms in Domleschg. He was the eldest son. But he
lost the farm with his gambling and drinking, and,
when the whole story of his wild extravagance came
out, his parents died of grief. He disappeared after
that and at first nobody knew where he had gone.
Some said he joined the army in Naples. No more
news came for about twelve to fifteen years. Then,
suddenly, he appeared again in Domleschg with an
almost grown-up boy and tried to find a home for
him with relations. But every door was closed
against him."

"That so embittered him that he vowed he would
never again set foot in Domleschg and came with
the boy to Dörfli to live. His wife must have been a
native of the Grisons. He probably met and married
her there and she died shortly afterwards. It seems
he still had a little money left—enough for the boy,
Tobias, to be apprenticed to a carpenter. He was a
good boy and well liked by everyone in Dörfli. But
nobody trusted the old man. There was a rumour
that he had to get out of Naples to avoid serious
trouble, because it was said that he had killed a
man—of course, not in the war, you understand,
but in some brawl. But we did not break our
connection with him since we were closely related.

My great-grand-mother on my mother's side was
his grandmother's sister, you know. We called him
'Uncle', and as we are related on my father's side to
almost everybody in Dörfli, the whole village called
him 'Uncle', too. And because he lived on the Alm
he was called the 'Alm-Uncle'."

"But what happened to Tobias?" asked Barbel
eagerly.

"Wait a moment, I am coming to that," replied
Dete. "Tobias served his apprenticeship in Mels,
and as soon as he had finished he came home to
Dörfli and married my sister, Adelheid. They were
very happy together, but their happiness was short-
lived. Two years later, while Tobias was working at
the building of a house, a beam fell on him and
killed him, and when his mutilated body was
brought home, Adelheid fell into a violent fever as a
result of the shock, and never recovered. In any
case, she was not very strong and sometimes took
strange fits when we couldn't tell whether she was
asleep or awake."

"Only a few weeks after Tobias died, Adelheid
too was buried. Some said it was the uncle's
punishment for the wicked life he had led, and they
even told him so to his face. The pastor, too,

begged him to repent of his past sins, but the uncle
only grew more fierce and embittered. He would
not speak to anyone, and everyone, in turn, kept
clear of him. Then we heard he had come to live on
the Alm and he has remained up there in solitude
ever since, at war with God and the world."

"Mother and I took in Adelheid's little child. She
was only a year old then. When Mother died last
summer and I had to go and work at the health
resort, I took the child with me and left her in
charge of old Ursel up in Pfaferserdorf. I was kept
on at the health resort during the winter, for I could
knit and sew and plenty of people gave me work to
do, and early in the spring some Frankfurt people I
had served during the summer came back. They
offered me a job, and I am going away with them to
Frankfurt. We leave the day after to-morrow."

"And you are going to leave the poor child with
that terrible old man!" said Barbel reproachfully.

"Well, what else can I do?" replied Dete defen-
sively. "I have done what I can for the child, and
can't take her with me. But, goodness! Where are
you going, Barbel? We are already half-way up the
Alm."

"I have almost come as far as I need," answered

Barbel. "I want to speak to Peter's grandmother.
She spins for me in winter. Goodbye, then, Dete!
And good luck!"

Dete shook her friend's hand and stopped while
Barbel walked towards the little brown Alm hut
which was situated in a sheltered spot some yards
off the path. The hut was more than half-way up the
Alm from the village. It was fortunate it stood in
such a sheltered place, for it looked dilapidated
beyond repair. Even situated as it was, it was hardly
safe to live in when gales swept the mountains.
Then everything in the hut, doors and windows and
all the old beams, would shake and crack.

The goat-herd lived here with his mother and his
old blind grand-mother. Peter was eleven years old.
Every morning he collected goats from the village
and drove them up to the Alm where they grazed till
evening. At sunset, Peter would go running nimbly
down the mountainside with his goats, until, on
reaching Dörfli he would whistle through his
fingers. The piercing sound summoned the owners
of the goats, who then took them home. Usually the
little boys and girls came to collect the animals, for
they were not in the least frightened of the gentle
goats, and this hour of the day, during the long

summer, was the time when Peter could see his
little friends. For the rest of the day he was alone on
the mountain with only the goat for company. He
often got home very late from Dörfli, for he stayed
as long as possible to play with his friends. So he
was left with just enough time to eat his bread and
milk, sleep and get up again early the next morning.
His father had been killed in a wood-cutting acci-
dent several years before. His mother, Brigitta, was
always called the goat-herd's wife, and his blind
grandmother was just "grandmother" to all and
sundry.

Dete stood looking impatiently in all directions to
catch a glimpse of the children and the goats; but
they had taken a very roundabout way. At first the
little girl had toiled hard to climb with the goat-herd,
panting in the heat and making a great effort under
her heavy encumbrance of clothes. She did not say a
word but looked steadily, now at Peter who jumped
about on his bare feet, now at the goats who climbed
still more easily on their slender little legs. Suddenly
the child sat down on the ground and quickly
removed her shoes and stockings. Then, standing
up, she began to take off her hot red shawl, then her
Sunday frock and her everyday frock, which Dete

had also made her wear, until, clad only in her light little petticoat, she stood with her bare arms stretched happily into the air. Then she put everything neatly into a little pile and jumped and climbed behind the goats. As she came skipping along in her new garb, Peter grinned broadly. He looked back, and when he saw the little pile of clothes lying on the path he grinned even more, but he said nothing. The child, feeling free at last, began to chatter to the boy, asking him how many goats he had, where he was going with them and what he would do there. So at last the children arrived at the cottage and caught sight of Aunt Dete. She no sooner spotted the group than she cried, "Heidi! What a sight you are! Where are your clothes? And the new shoes I bought you, and the stockings I knitted? Where have you put them?"

The child quietly pointed down the hill.

The aunt followed the direction of her finger. There was, indeed, something lying on the ground. "You dreadful child!" she cried in great annoyance. "What's the meaning of this? Why have you taken everything off?"

"I didn't need them," said the child, not looking at all penitent.

"Oh, have you no sense?" lamented the aunt. "Who is to go back down for them? It's all of half an hour's walk." Then turning to Peter, she ordered, "Peter! Run back and fetch the clothes!"

"I am late already," said Peter slowly, and remained motionless, both hands in his pockets.

"Don't just stand there staring!" Aunt Dete cried. "This will never do! Come here! I will give you something good. Look!" And she held up a bright new coin. The boy's eyes shone at the sight of it. Suddenly he jumped up and made off down the Alm by the shortest way. Soon he reached the little pile of clothes, gathered them up and sped back so quickly that the aunt could not but be pleased, and at once gave him the coin. Peter put it in his pocket, his face wreathed in smiles for he didn't often come by such a prize.

"You can take the clothes up to the uncle's since you are going that way," Aunt Dete said as she started to climb the steep slope which rose just behind Goat Peter's cottage. Readily Peter carried out the order and followed as she walked ahead; his left arm round the bundle, the goats' stick swinging in his right hand. Heidi and the goats leaped joyously at his side. Thus, in three quarters of an hour, the little group reached the top of the Alm where the old uncle's cottage stood on a ledge of the mountain. Behind the hut were three ancient fir trees, and beyond these, the mountain rose in an almost sheer wall, the lower parts still overgrown with grasses and flowers, with stonier slopes above leading to the black, bare, jagged peaks. Along the side of the cottage facing the valley, the uncle had made himself a bench, and here he now sat puffing his pipe, both hands on his knees, calmly watching the children, the goats and Aunt Dete as they climbed. Heidi arrived first. She went straight up to the old man, stretched out her hand towards him and said, "Good evening, Grandfather!"

"Well, well! What is the meaning of this?" asked the old man gruffly. He took the child's hand abruptly and as he did so a long, piercing glance shot from beneath his bushy eyebrows. Heidi returned his look without blinking. The grandfather presented a fearsome aspect. His face seemed covered in beard and eyebrows, and Heidi could not take her fascinated gaze away from him.

In the meantime, the aunt and Peter had arrived.

"I wish you good day!" said Dete shortly. "This is Tobias' and Adelheid's child. You will hardly recognise her because you have not seen her since she was a year old."

"What have I to do with the child?" asked the old man brusquely. "And you, there!" he called to Peter. "Take yourself off with your goats! You are late as it is."

Peter obeyed at once, for the uncle had given him an angry look which did not make him wish to linger.

"The child just has to stay with you, Uncle," said Dete. "I have done my bit for four years. Now it is your turn."

"Indeed!" mumbled the old man, his glance flashing at Dete. "And if the child starts fretting for you as children do, being such difficult things, what shall I do with her then?"

"That's up to you," replied Dete. "No one told me what to do with the little one when she was left in my care, and only one year old, too. Now I have to make my own living and you are the child's nearest relative. If you can't look after her it's your responsibility and you must answer for any harm that comes to her. And I shouldn't think you can afford to add another to your list of wicked deeds."

At that point Dete realised she had said more than she should have.

At her words, the old man got up. He looked so threatening that she took a step backwards. Flinging out his arm, he shouted at her, "Be off! And don't be in a hurry to show your face here again!"

Dete did not need a second telling. "Good-bye, then!" she said hurriedly. "And you, too, Heidi!" And with that she turned and ran down the mountain, and didn't stop until she reached Dörfli.

This time, people were even more eager to stop and question her, wondering what had become of the child. They all knew Dete well, and also the history of the child. When voices called from every door and window, "Where is the child, Dete? What have you done with her?" she replied angrily, "With the Alm-Uncle, of course! I left her with the Alm-Uncle, just as I said." The women of the village began to cry out at her: "Shame on you for leaving a little girl up there! What a terrible thing to do."

Dete ran through the village as fast as she could go. Her one thought was to get away from Dörfli and to avoid speaking to any one, for she was far from easy in her conscience about what she had done. The child's dying mother had asked Dete to take care of Heidi, and here she was, abandoning the girl to an unknown fate. However, she consoled herself with the thought of being better able to provide for the child with her newly earned money, and with the wonderful prospect of soon being free to enjoy her new position far away from all the village talk.

CHAPTER 2

The Grandfather's Hut

Long after Dete had gone, the grandfather went back to his seat outside the hut, and sat silently blowing clouds of smoke from his pipe while Heidi began to inspect her new surroundings. She found a shed, attached to one side of the hut, which housed the goats. She peeped in and then walked round to the other side of the cottage where there stood three old fir trees. A strong wind shook their thick branches and the child stood still, listening to the moaning of the wind in the ancient trees. Then she completed the circuit of the cottage and returned to where the grandfather sat. He hadn't moved an inch since she'd left him, so she went across and stood in front of him, her hands clasped behind her back, her steady eyes looking at him.

The old man raised his head. Heidi stayed where she was and continued to gaze at him. "Well, what are we going to do now" he said.

"I would like to see inside the cottage."

"Come, then!" The grandfather got up. "And bring your bundle of clothes!"

"I don't need them any more," declared Heidi.

The old man turned and looked searchingly at the child. Heidi's dark eyes were shining with delight at the prospect of seeing inside the cottage. "She doesn't lack sense, anyway," he said quietly to himself. Then, "Why don't you need them any more?" he asked aloud.

"I would rather be dressed like the goats with their bare legs."

"All right, then, but bring the things!" commanded the grandfather. "We will put them in the cupboard."

Heidi obediently picked up her bundle and followed the old man inside. The door opened directly on to a big room which was the full breadth of the cottage. The only furniture in the room was a table and a chair. In one corner stood the grandfather's bed and in the opposite wall the fireplace above which hung a big kettle. On the same side as the bed, in the middle of the wall, there was a door which the grandfather now opened. This was the cupboard where he kept his belongings. On a shelf lay a couple of shirts, socks and some rough sack-cloth sheets. On another stood plates, cups and glasses, and on the top shelf there was a round loaf, a sausage, ham and cheese. Everything that Alm-Uncle possessed in the way of food and clothing was kept in this cupboard. As soon as the door was opened Heidi came forward and pushed her own clothes as far behind the grandfather's as possible so that they would be well out of the way. Then she turned her attention to the room and asked, "Where shall I sleep, Grandfather?"

"Wherever you want to."

This seemed to please the child and she began to inspect every corner. By the grandfather's bed, wooden steps went up, and when the child climbed the little ladder she found herself in the hayloft. A bale of hay, fresh and sweet-smelling, lay on the floor, and from a little window in the roof she could see far down into the valley.

"Oh, this is where I want to sleep!" she cried joyfully. "It is lovely! Come and see how lovely it is, Grandfather!"

"I have seen it before!" came from below.

"I am going to make my bed," the child called again and ran busily to and fro. "You must bring me a sheet to lie upon, Grandfather!"

"Indeed!" remarked the grandfather, and after a while he went to the cupboard and raked about amongst the clothes. Presently he pulled out a long, coarse piece of sack-cloth which might serve as a sheet. He carried it up to the loft and there he saw that a very nice little bed had been made amongst the hay, with extra hay piled up into a pillow at one end, and arranged in such a way that whoever lay on the improvised bed would be able to look up at the little window.

"Well done!" exclaimed the grandfather. "Now the sheet goes on. But wait——I" and here he took a big bunch of hay and made the bed twice as thick so that the hardness of the floor would not come through.

"Now bring it here!"

Heidi quickly grasped the sheet but it was so thick and heavy, she staggered under the weight, It was just as well though, as the thickness of the cloth would prevent the sharp stalks of hay from sticking into her. Together they spread the sheet and now the bed looked very trim and tidy; but Heidi stood back and regarded it critically.

"There is still something we have forgotten, Grandfather."

"Now what?" he asked.

"A top sheet. When you get into bed you need something to pull over you."

"Oh, indeed! But what if I haven't got any?"

"Don't worry, Grandfather," Heidi consoled him. "We can use more hay for a cover," and she began to gather another bundle.

"Wait a moment!" The old man went down the steps to his own bed. Back he came presently with a big, heavy, linen sack which he laid on the floor.

"Isn't that better than hay?" he asked, helping her to spread it on the bed, for Heidi's little frame couldn't manage to lift and spread the heavy cover out smoothly.

Heidi stood admiringly before her new sleeping-place. "The cover is beautiful!" she declared ecstatically, "and the bed is just perfect! I wish it were night-time already so that I could go to sleep on it!"

"I think we should eat first," the grandfather advised.

In her eagerness, Heidi had forgotten everything

except the new bed, but now, when she thought of it, she did indeed feel very hungry, for she had had nothing to eat since that morning before the journey, when she had breakfasted meagerly on a piece of bread and a small cup of watery coffee. "Yes, I think so, too!" she agreed.

"Well, then, since we are in such complete agreement, let's go down," said the old man, guiding the child towards the stairs.

In the room below he went over to the fireplace, pushed back the big kettle and brought a little one forward on the chain. Then he sat down on a three-legged stool and blew up the fire. It was soon blazing merrily and the little kettle began to boil. Next the old man cut a big piece of cheese, and piercing it with a long, iron fork, he held it over the fire, turning it constantly to and fro until it was golden brown all over. Heidi had watched all these operations with the closest attention and apparently some new ideas had entered her head for suddenly she jumped up and went to the cupboard. When the grandfather had decided that the cheese was nicely toasted and took it to the table, there was the round loaf, two plates and two knives neatly laid, for Heidi had been quick to see what was wanted and had brought everything from the cupboard.

"So you can think for yourself! That's good!" said the grandfather and spread the toasted cheese on the bread. "But there is still something missing."

Heidi's eyes alighted on the steaming pot by the fire and she knew at once what it was. Quickly she ran back to the cupboard but could find only one little bowl. She hesitated only a moment for right at the back were two glasses. Presently she came back and put the little bowl and glasses on the table.

"Very good! Very good!" said the old man. "You have found a way out of the difficulty. But now, where are *you* going to sit?" and he drew his own chair up to the table.

Heidi ran to the hearth and brought back the little three-legged stool.

"You have got a seat, at any rate," said the grandfather, "though it is rather low! Even on my chair you would be too small to reach the table. But now you must eat. Come along!"

He filled the little bowl with milk and placing it on his own chair pushed it near the stool so that Heidi had a little table of her own. Then he filled a plate with a big piece of bread and some of the

yellow, toasted cheese and laid it also on the chair.
He himself sat on the corner of the table and began
his meal. Heidi lifted her little bowl and drank without stopping. Then she drew a deep breath—for she
had been so thirsty that she hadn't even stopped to
breathe—and put down the empty bowl.

"Do you like the milk?" the grandfather asked.

"It is the best milk I have ever tasted!" replied
Heidi.

"You can have more," said the grandfather, filling the little bowl again and putting it before her.
She spread the bread with her slice of golden cheese
and began eating hungrily.

The cheese was soft as butter and tasted good.
From time to time Heidi took a drink from the bowl
and looked blissfully happy.

When the meal was finished, the grandfather
went out to the goat-house where there was work to
be done. Heidi watched him attentively, observing
how he first swept everything clean with the broom
then spread fresh straw for the little animals to sleep
on. At last the goat-house was finished and he went
into the shed which was close by. Here he chopped
several round sticks to equal lengths; then he carefully shaped a flat piece of wood and drilled four

holes into one side. He put the round sticks into the holes—and there was a chair like the grandfather's, only much higher! Speechless with admiration, Heidi gazed at it.

"What do you think it is, Heidi?" asked the grandfather.

"It is *my* chair, because it is so high. But you made it so quickly, Grandfather!" said the little girl in amazement.

"She has eyes in her head all right," thought the grandfather as he walked round the cottage, fixing a loose board at the door and repairing anything that needed attention. Heidi followed close behind. Nothing escaped her notice, and everything she saw gave her new pleasure.

Evening came, and the old fir trees behind the cottage began to rustle more loudly as a strong wind swept along, roaring amongst the branches. Heidi's heart beat faster. She thought she had never heard anything so beautiful and went skipping and running for sheer joy under the trees. All the while the grandfather watched the child from the doorway.

There was the sound of a shrill whistle. Heidi stood still and the grandfather stepped out of the

cottage. From above, the goats came jumping like
wild creatures and in the midst of them was Peter.
With a joyful cry, Heidi rushed to welcome her old
friends of the morning. At the cottage, children and
animals came to a halt and two pretty, slender
goats, one brown, one white, ran from the herd
towards the grandfather. Eagerly they licked his
hands for in the palms he held a little salt which the
goats liked very much. Peter disappeared with the
rest of the flock and Heidi fell to caressing first one
and then the other of the goats and jumped gaily
round them.

"Do they belong to us, Grandfather? Do they
really belong to us?" she asked. "Will they stay in
the little shed? Do they always stay with us?" Heidi
scarcely gave the grandfather a chance to put in his
steady, "Yes! Yes!" between one question and the
next.

When the goats had finished licking the salt from
his hands, the old man commanded, "Go and fetch
your little bowl and the bread!"

Heidi obeyed at once. Then the grandfather
milked the white goat into the little bowl which was
soon full to the brim. He cut a piece of bread and
handing it to the child said, "Eat now, and then go

upstairs to sleep. I suppose your night things are in
the bundle Aunt Dete made up, which I put in the
cupboard. Get it out if you need it. I have to tie up
the goats for the night. Sleep well!"

"Good night, Grandfather! But what are the
goats' names? Tell me, Grandfather!" cried the
child, running behind the old man's receding
figure.

"The white one is called 'Little Swan' and the
brown one is 'Little Bear'," the grandfather called
over his shoulder.

"Good night, Little Swan! Good night, Little
Bear!" cried Heidi happily as all three disappeared
into the goat-house.

Heidi went back to the bench outside the cottage
where she sat and took her bread and milk. The
wind was so strong she was almost blown from her
seat, so she finished hurriedly and went into the
house and upstairs to bed where she was soon fast
asleep, as soundly and happily as though on the
best feather-bed. Not long after, and before the
darkness had come completely, the grandfather,
too, had gone to bed, for he always rose at sunrise,
which was at a very early hour during the long
summer months. All night long the wind blew

strongly so that the whole cottage seemed to shake and every beam cracked and groaned.

In the middle of the night the grandfather rose, saying half aloud to himself, "Perhaps she is afraid." He climbed the steps and stood by Heidi's bed. At intervals the moon shone brightly, then as clouds were chased across it everything became dark again. At that moment a shaft of moonlight came through the little window, falling directly on Heidi's bed. Her cheeks were flushed from sleep and her head rested quietly and peacefully on her little round arm. Her dreams appeared to be happy ones for a smile played about her mouth. The grandfather gazed at the sleeping child until the moon was again overshadowed. Then he went back to his bed.

CHAPTER 3

On the Alm

Early in the morning, Heidi was awakened by a loud whistle. As she opened her eyes, a gleam of sunshine came through the little window on to her bed and shone on the hay nearby so that everything was bathed in golden light. Then, from outside, she heard the grandfather's deep, quiet voice and she remembered that she was up on the Alm. She no longer lived with old Ursel who was almost stone deaf and always wanted to have Heidi by her side, so that sometimes the child had felt like a prisoner and would have liked to run away from the stuffy room where she had to sit all day. For Ursel was always too cold and insisted on keeping the room unbearably hot. So Heidi was very glad when she awoke and found herself in her new

home. She remembered all the exciting things she
had seen the previous day and wondered what this
new day had in store for her. Above all she looked
forward to seeing Little Swan and Little Bear again.
Quickly she jumped out of bed and in a few minutes
had dressed herself. Then she climbed down the
steps and ran out to the front of the cottage. Peter,
the goat-herd, was already there with his flock and
the grandfather was leading out Little Swan and
Little Bear to join them. Heidi ran forward to say
good-morning to him and the goats.

"How would you like to go with them to the
pasture?" asked the grandfather.

Heidi was overjoyed. That was the thing she
would like best of all.

"But first you must wash yourself or the sun,
shining brightly up there, will laugh at you when he
looks down and sees how dirty you are! See! This is
where you wash." The grandfather pointed towards
a big flat tub filled with water which stood in the
sun before the cottage door. Heidi jumped towards
it and splashed and scrubbed until she was perfectly
clean. In the meantime the grandfather went into
the cottage, calling to Peter, "Come here, goat-
general, and bring your rucksack!"

Amazed, Peter answered the call and laid down the rucksack in which he carried his meagre lunch.

"Open it!" ordered the old man, and then put in a big piece of bread and an equally big piece of cheese. Peter opened his round eyes very wide for this food was twice as much as he had for his own lunch.

"And now the little bowl has to go in, too," the old man continued. "At lunch-time you will milk for her two little bowlfuls, for she is going, too, and can stay with you until you come back in the evening. Take care she doesn't fall over the precipice!"

Now Heidi came running towards them. "Grandfather, the sun can't laugh at me now!" For fear of the sun's mockery she had rubbed her face, neck and arms so vigorously with the rough cloth which the grandfather had hung up beside the water-tub, that she was almost as red as a lobster.

The old man smiled. "No, he has no reason to laugh now," he agreed. "But do you know what happens when you come home in the evening? You go right into the tub like a fish because if you run like the goats your feet will get dirty. Now, off you go!"

Happily the children climbed up the Alm. The
high winds during the night had blown away the last
little cloud and now the sky was a vast expanse of
deep blue out of which the sun shone and glittered
on the green slopes. The little blue and yellow
mountain flowers opened their cups and seemed to
nod merrily at Heidi who romped everywhere. Here
and there were big patches of pretty red primroses,
and china-blue gentians, and enchanted by this
sparkling, waving sea of flowers, she forgot all about
Peter, even about the goats. All along the way she
picked flowers until she had a big bunch which she
wrapped in her pinafore, for she wanted to take
them home and put them in her bedroom, so that it
would look as pretty as the fields themselves.

Peter was quite dazed trying to look in every
direction at once, for the goats, like Heidi, were
jumping from one place to another. He had to whistle and shout and brandish his stick to bring the
goats together again.

"Where are you now, Heidi?" came the boy's
exasperated and rather angry cry.

"Here!" came the reply, but Peter could see no
one. Heidi was sitting, hidden from view, behind a
little hillock which was covered with sweet-smelling

prunella. The air was filled with the perfume of
these beautiful flowers, and Heidi was sitting taking
in deep breaths of the scented air and thinking how
wonderful it all was.

"Come here!" Peter called again. "You are not to
go near the precipice—the uncle said so!"

"Where is that?" asked Heidi, still not moving
from her hiding-place.

"Up there! Right on the top the old eagle sits on
the look-out for his prey."

That did the trick.

At once Heidi jumped up and ran to Peter with
her apronful of flowers.

"That is enough flower-picking for now," he said
as they climbed up together, "if you are going to
keep pace with me. And if you pick all the flowers
to-day there will be none left for to-morrow."

Heidi was convinced. Moreover, her pinafore
was so full that it could hardly hold another one. So
she now walked quietly beside Peter. The goats
were also quieter, as they were anxious to reach
their delicious pasture, and climbed unhesitatingly
towards their grazing ground. The pasture which
Peter usually chose and where he spent the day was
situated at the foot of the high rocks. Bushes and fir

trees covered the lower parts but nearer the summit the rocks rose bare and rugged towards the sky. On one side of the mountain, jagged clefts stretched far down and the grandfather had been right to warn Peter of the danger. When they had reached the pasture, Peter carefully put his rucksack into a little hollow in the ground, for the wind often blew with great violence across this part of the country and Peter did not want to see his precious possessions rolling down the mountainside. Then the boy, tired after the strenuous climb, stretched himself out at full length on the sunny pasture.

Heidi, by this time, had undone her pinafore and rolled it neatly round the flowers which she laid beside Peter's rucksack in the hollow. Then she sat down beside him and looked around. The valley lay far below, bathed in the sparkling morning sunshine. In front of Heidi a big, broad snowfield rose up to the dark blue sky and on the left stood a huge pile of rocks above which a bare rocky peak reached towards the sky, towering majestically above the child. Heidi sat motionless. A great silence was all around and only the delicate blue harebells and yellow cistus swayed softly in the gentle breeze, nodding joyfully on their slender little stems. Peter had fallen asleep and the goats were climbing high up amongst the bushes. Heidi had never been so happy. The golden sunlight, the fresh breezes and the delicate perfume of the flowers filled her with delight and she only wished that she might stay there for ever. She gazed so long at the mountains that it seemed to her that each had a face and that these mountain faces were as familiar to her as old friends.

Suddenly Heidi heard a loud, harsh cry and when she looked up she saw, circling overhead, a huge bird, larger than she had ever seen before. His large wings were outspread and he flew in a wide circle, coming back again and again and uttering loud, piercing shrieks above Heidi's head.

"Peter! Peter! Wake up!" cried Heidi. "Look! There is a big bird just above us!"

Peter got up and watched the bird, too, as it rose higher and higher and at last disappeared behind the grey rocks.

"Where has he gone to?" asked Heidi who had been watching the bird with keen interest.

"Home to his nest," replied Peter.

"Is his home up there? Oh, how nice to live so high up! How terrible he cries! Let's climb up there and see where his nest is!"

"Oh, no!" replied Peter emphatically. "Even the goats can't climb so high and the uncle said you were not to climb the rocks."

Suddenly Peter started to whistle and call loudly. Heidi could not think what this meant, but the goats apparently understood, for, one after another, they came springing down until they were all gathered together on the green slope. Some continued to nibble and others ran about, playfully pushing each other with their horns. Heidi jumped up and ran amongst them. She delighted in their individual antics and quickly made friends with each of them in turn, for to her they were like separate people with their own personalities. While she played with the goats Peter fetched the rucksack and laid out the four pieces of bread on the ground, the big ones on Heidi's side and the small ones on his own. Then he took the little bowl, drew some milk into it from Little Swan and placed it in the centre. "Stop skipping now! It is time to eat," he said. But he had to shout again, for Heidi was so absorbed in her games with the goats that she was oblivious to everything else. So Peter called until the rocks themselves echoed his voice, and then Heidi appeared and ran to join

Peter and the feast spread out on the ground before him.

She sat down. "Is the milk for me?" she asked.

"Yes," replied Peter, "and the two big pieces of bread and cheese are yours too, and when you have finished you get another bowlful from Little Swan."

"And where do you get your milk?" asked Heidi.

"From my own goat. Go on and eat," urged Peter.

Heidi began to drink her milk and as soon as she put down her empty bowl Peter filled it again. Then Heidi gave a big piece of her bread to Peter and all the cheese as well, saying, "You can have it all. I have had enough."

Peter gazed at her, speechless with surprise. Never in his life could he have given away as much as that. He hesitated a little, for he could not believe that Heidi meant it seriously. She held out the pieces, but as Peter still did not take them she laid the food on his knees. Peter had never before had such a satisfying lunch.

The animals had begun to climb up again towards the bushes; some skipping gaily over everything, others stopping to taste the tender herbs. Heidi watched the goats, and after a while she said, "Tell me their names, Peter."

Peter knew them all, of course, and told Heidi the name of each, pointing them out as he did so. Heidi listened carefully and very soon she had learnt their names off by heart and could call to each one, for they all had distinguishing characteristics.

Turk was the big one, with enormous horns with which he was always trying to butt the others. So he was mostly left on his own as the rest of them were frightened of his bullying.

Only one, little Goldfinch, would face him without fear, and would rush at him nimbly, several times, so that Turk simply stood still in bewilderment, not knowing which way to turn, for her little horns were sharp.

There was also a sad little goat called White Snowflake, who bleated plaintively, and Heidi had frequently to go and comfort it and stroke its little soft head. Just then, it cried again, and Heidi ran over, and clasping her arms around it, beseeched it to tell her what was wrong. The goat snuggled to Heidi and stopped bleating.

Peter called out, between mouthfuls of bread and cheese, "She is missing her mother, an old goat who was sold at Mayenfeld the other day."

"Hasn't she a grandfather or a grandmother?" called back Heidi.

"She has neither," replied Peter.

"Oh, poor Snowflake," cried Heidi. "Please don't cry any more; I will come with you every day, and I will never leave you alone again, I promise."

The young goat nuzzled Heidi's shoulder and seemed more content.

Peter now joined Heidi, who had come to the conclusion that the best and most distinctive goats by far were the two which were owned by her grandfather. They even treated the arrogant Turk with total indifference.

"Peter," Heidi said presently, "the prettiest of all are Little Swan and Little Bear." These two were light on their feet, and always seemed to find the best leaves to nibble. Heidi watched them with pleasure.

"I know," Peter replied. "The uncle brushes and washes them, and gives them salt, and has the nicest shed."

Suddenly Peter jumped up and bounded after the goats. Heidi followed. Something must have happened and she simply could not stay behind. Peter forced his way through the middle of the herd to that side of the Alm where the bare and jagged rocks fell away steeply. Here, a heedless little goat might easily tumble down and break his legs. Peter had noticed inquisitive little Goldfinch jumping in that direction. The boy arrived just in time, for the little goat was just about to jump towards the edge of the precipice. Peter, lunging towards the goat, fell down and only managed to seize one of its legs as he fell. Goldfinch gave an angry cry at finding herself caught and tried desperately to free herself. Peter could not get up and shouted for Heidi to help because he was afraid Goldfinch might wrench her leg. Heidi was already there and at once saw the danger. She quickly gathered some sweet-smelling plants from the ground and held them out towards Goldfinch, saying coaxingly, "Come along, Goldfinch, and be good! Look! You might fall down and hurt yourself."

The little goat turned quickly and ate the herbs from Heidi's outstretched hand. In the meantime Peter got to his feet again and held Goldfinch by the cord with which her little bell was fastened to her neck. Heidi grasped the goat in the same way at the other side of its head and together they led the truant back to the peacefully grazing flock. As soon as Peter got her back to safety, he raised his stick and started to give her a good beating. Goldfinch, however, knowing what was in store, timidly shrank back, and Heidi cried, "No, Peter! No! You mustn't beat her! Look how frightened she is!"

"She deserves it," Peter muttered, about to strike; but Heidi threw herself against his arm, crying indignantly, "Don't touch her! You will hurt her! Leave her alone!"

Peter turned surprised eyes on the fierce little girl and his stick dropped to his side. "All right, then, I'll let her off—if you give me some of your cheese to-morrow again," he bargained.

"You can have it all, to-morrow and every day. I don't want it," Heidi consented. "And I'll give you the bread, too, the same as today, but you must promise never to beat Goldfinch or Snowflake, or any of the goats."

"Suits me," said Peter, and that was as good as a promise. He let Goldfinch go and the little goat leapt joyously towards the herd.

So the day passed quickly and the sun began to sink behind the mountains. Heidi was sitting quietly on the ground, gazing at the cistus and the harebells which glistened in the evening sunshine; rocks and grass shimmered in a golden glow. Suddenly she jumped up and cried, "Peter! Peter! They are on fire! They are all on fire! All the mountains are burning! And the great snow mountain also, and the sky! Oh, look at the lovely fiery snow! Peter, get up and look! The fire is at the great bird's nest, too. Look at the rocks and the grass and the fir trees! Everything is on fire!"

"It is always like that," replied Peter with great unconcern, continuing to peel his stick, "but it is not real fire."

"What is it, then?" asked Heidi, gazing eagerly around. She ran back and forth looking from side to side, as if she could not take in enough of the majestic sight. "What is it, Peter?"

"It just gets like that," Peter tried to explain.

"Oh, look, look, Peter!" cried Heidi again in great excitement. "Everything is turning a rosy pink colour. Look at the snow and the high rocks! What are their names Peter"

"Mountains don't have names," replied Peter.

"Oh, how beautiful. Crimson snow! Oh, now all the rocks are turning grey—now the colour is all gone. Now it is all over, Peter."

Heidi sat down, looking as distressed as if everything really had come to an end.

"To-morrow it will be the same," said Peter. "Get up now. We must go home."

"Will it be like this every day we are on the pasture?" asked Heidi insistently, as she walked down the Alm at Peter's side. She waited breathlessly for his answer, hoping that he would be able to set her mind at rest.

"Mostly," he replied. "But will it definitely be like that again tomorrow" Heidi persisted. "Yes, yes; it will certainly come tomorrow," Peter replied.

Heidi was very happy. She had absorbed so many new impressions . . . had so many new things to think about that she was quite silent until they reached the hut and saw the grandfather sitting on the bench under the fir trees. Here he sat in the evenings, waiting for his goats.

Heidi ran up to him, followed by Little Swan and Little Bear, for the goats knew their master.

"Good night!" Peter called after Heidi, and then added, "come again, tomorrow!" because he was very anxious for her to go with him. Heidi ran back and gave her hand to Peter, promising him that she would go with him, and then ran over to little Snowflake, whom she clasped gently round the neck, saying, "Sleep well, and don't forget that I will be back tomorrow, so you needn't be sad." Snowflake looked at her happily and then leapt off after the other goats.

Heidi raced towards her grandfather.

"Oh, Grandfather, it was wonderful" she cried long before she reached him. "The fire on the snow and the rocks and the blue and yellow flowers, and look what I have brought for you!" Heidi unfolded her pinafore and all the flowers fell at the grandfather's feet. But what a sight the poor flowers were! Heidi did not recognise them. They were like withered grass and not a single little cup was open.

"Grandfather, what is the matter with the flowers?"
cried Heidi, quite alarmed. "They weren't like that
before. What is wrong with them?"

"They would rather be out in the sun than tied
up in a pinafore," explained the grandfather.

"Then I will never gather any more. But
Grandfather, why did the eagle screech so?" Heidi
asked.

"You had better have your bath now," said the
grandfather, "and I shall fetch some milk from the
shed. Afterwards, when we are having our supper, I
will tell you about everything."

Later, when Heidi sat in her high chair, the little
bowl of milk in front of her and the grandfather at
her side, she again asked her question.

"Why did the great bird scream at us,
Grandfather?"

"He screams in mockery of the people in the
villages down in the valley where they sit gossiping
together. He wants to say, 'If you would all mind
your own business or climb up into the heights like
me you would be much happier!'"

The grandfather spoke these words with such
vehemence that Heidi seemed to hear again the
croaking of the great bird.

"Why don't the mountains have names, Grandfather?" asked Heidi again.

"They have names," he answered, "and if you can describe one to me so that I can recognise it, then I will tell you its name."

Heidi tried to describe the rocky mountain with the two high peaks exactly as she had seen it. Presently the grandfather interrupted, "Yes, I know that one. Its name is Falknis. Did you notice any others?"

Then Heidi recalled the mountain with the large snowfield which looked at first as if it were on fire and then turned rose-coloured, then pale pink, and at last faded back to its own grey colour.

"I know that one, too," said the grandfather. "That is the Scesaplana. Did you like being on the pasture?"

Now Heidi told him everything: how wonderful it had been and particularly about the fire in the evening. Heidi wanted the grandfather to explain why this had happened, since Peter had been unable to do so.

"You see," the grandfather instructed her, "that's what the sun does when he says good night to the mountains. He throws his most beautiful rays over them so that they won't forget him before morning."

Heidi was delighted. She could hardly wait for the next day when she would again be allowed to go to the pasture, to watch how the sun said good night to the mountains. But first she had to go to bed, and how soundly she slept all night on her hay bed and dreamt of nothing but glistening mountains tinged with red, and Little Snowflake running happily about!

CHAPTER 4

Peter's Grandmother

Next morning, the sun shone brightly as Peter appeared with the goats and they all went up together to the pasture. And so it continued every day. Heidi grew stronger and sturdier with living so much in the open and her little sunburnt face shone with health. When autumn came and the wind blew with greater force over the mountains, the grandfather would sometimes say, "To-day you had better stay at home, Heidi. A little one like you might easily be swept down the mountainside by the wind."

But when Peter heard this in the morning he would look very miserable. He found it dull now without Heidi; and, of course, he got less to eat. On such days the goats would become so stubborn that he had twice as much trouble with them. They, too, had grown so accustomed to Heidi that they would hardly move off without her.

Heidi herself was never bored because she always saw something new and exciting to take up her attention. Best of all she liked to go up the Alm with the goats to where the great bird was, where there was such a lot to see, and so much to experience with the little goats and their different personalities. But she also liked to watch the grandfather at work, helping him all she could at the carpenter's bench.

Then a very special treat for Heidi was to watch the grandfather prepare the lovely round goat's milk cheese. But even in the midst of such exciting activities she would sometimes steal away when the wind blew strongest to stand and listen beneath the old fir trees, catching her breath as the wind roared amongst the branches. Nothing sounded so strange and mysterious to her as the stirring of the tree-tops. She would stand directly beneath them and look up at the bending, swaying, roaring branches, bowing to the mighty wind sweeping through them.

As the season changed, the sun lost the fierce heat of summer and Heidi looked out her warm stockings and shoes and her wool dress. Gradually

the weather grew colder and as Heidi stood beneath
the trees, she would feel as if the wind were blowing
straight through her, but she could never tear
herself away and go indoors while the stirring
branches beckoned her. As it grew ever colder,
Peter would appear early in the morning blowing
on his hands to warm them. Then one morning
they awoke to find the whole Alm covered in snow.
Not one blade of grass was visible. Peter and the
goats did not appear and Heidi watched from the
window of the hut as the big snowflakes fell. The
snow fell thickly until it reached above the window
so that it was impossible to open it and Heidi and
the Alm-Uncle were imprisoned in the hut. This
amused Heidi and she ran from one window to
another expecting the hut to be covered right over
at any moment. The next day it had stopped snow-
ing and the grandfather forced his way out and
shovelled the snow away from around the hut. Soon
the snow was heaped up around the cottage and
they were able to open the window again. In the
afternoon, as Heidi and the grandfather sat together
by the fire there came a great thumping outside the
door. At last the door opened and there stood
Peter, knocking the snow from his boots. He had

struggled through deep snowdrifts and he still had great lumps of frozen snow clinging to his clothes.

"Good evening!" he said coming in and at once getting as near as possible to the fire. After this salutation the boy lapsed into complete silence but nevertheless his whole face beamed with joy.

Heidi looked at him in amazement for the snow which had covered him from head to foot was beginning to melt and ran from him in rivulets.

"Well, General, and how are things going?" called the grandfather. "Now that the goat army has been disbanded you will have to turn to nibbling at the slate pencil."

"Why must he nibble the slate pencil?" asked Heidi at once.

"In winter the boy has to go to school," explained the grandfather. "There he learns to read and write and that is sometimes difficult; and then it helps a little if one can nibble the slate pencil, isn't that so, General?"

"Yes, that's true," acknowledged Peter.

Now Heidi's interest was thoroughly aroused. She asked Peter many questions about school and everything to be seen and heard there. Since conversation with Peter was inclined to be a slow business he had ample opportunity to get thoroughly dry. He always had great difficulty in putting his thoughts into words and on the subject of school this was particularly hard. By the time he had managed to think of the answer to one question Heidi had already thought of two or three more to ask and they were all of a kind which required much answering. The grandfather kept silent during this dialogue but an occasional twitch of amusement at the corners of his mouth showed that he was listening.

"Well, General, now you have been under fire and must be in need of some refreshment!" As he spoke, the old man rose and got the supper from the cupboard and Heidi brought the chairs up to the table. The grandfather had also made a bench for two people, hinged into the wall, and several different seats here and there, so that he and Heidi could sit together, as she had a way of staying close beside him whatever he was doing. So there was plenty of room for all of them to sit in comfort.

Peter's round eyes opened wider when he saw what a large piece of delicious meat the grandfather put on his plate. He had not enjoyed himself so much for a long time. As they finished the meal it began to grow dark and Peter prepared to go home. He had already bade them good night, but turned again at the door and said: "I'll come back again on Sunday, a week to-day, but the-grandmother said she would like you to come to see her some time."

This new idea of going to visit somebody appealed to Heidi at once and on the following morning her first words were, "Grandfather, I must go down and see the grandmother today. She will be expecting me."

"The snow is too deep," replied the grandfather to put her off. But Heidi was determined to go since she had got the grandmother's message. Not a day passed without her pleading, "Grandfather, I must go now! The grandmother is waiting for me!"

On the fourth day a hard frost had set in and the ground cracked at every step. But the bright sun peeped in at the window and fell on Heidi where she sat on her high chair at the table. Soon she had begun her customary little speech, "Today I must go to the grandmother or she will be tired of waiting for me."

The grandfather rose and going up to the hayloft brought down the thick sack which was Heidi's bedcover. "Come, then!" he said. Joyously the child skipped out into the glittering snow world. The old fir trees were silent now and on every branch the snow lay thickly.

The grandfather went into the shed and brought out a large sleigh. There was a pole fixed at the side and from the low seat the sleigh could be guided by the feet pressing against the ground and with the help of the pole.

The grandfather took his seat on the sleigh and placed the child on his knee, wrapping her carefully in the sack to keep her warm. His left arm held her secure and this was necessary for the long drive ahead. Then he grasped the pole with his right hand and gave a push with his feet. The sleigh shot down the Alm with such rapidity that Heidi felt she was flying through the air like a bird. She shouted aloud with joy.

By and by the sleigh stopped with a jerk just outside Goat Peter's cottage. The grandfather lifted the child and unwrapped her, saying, "Now in you go and when it starts to get dark come straight home!" Then he turned and pulled the sleigh back up the mountain.

Heidi opened the cottage door and found herself

in a small, rather dark room. She could see a fire-place and a shelf with some dishes so she concluded that this was the kitchen. Then she saw a door and she found that it led into another, narrower room. This cottage was quite different from her grandfa-ther's and everything looked very poor and shabby. When Heidi entered the room she saw a table, and at the table a woman was sitting patching a jacket which Heidi recognised at once as Peter's. In the corner, an old bent woman sat spinning. Heidi went straight to her. "Good day, Grandmother!" she said. "Here I am to see you. Did you think I was long in coming?"

The old woman lifted her head and groped for the hand which Heidi held out to her. When she had found it she held it for a while, thoughtfully. Then she said, "Are you the child who stays with the Alm-Uncle? Are you Heidi?"

"Yes," said Heidi. "I have just come down in the sleigh with Grandfather."

"How can it be? Your hands are quite warm. Brigitta, did the Alm-Uncle himself come with the child?"

Peter's mother, Brigitta, who had been mending at the table got up and looked curiously at the little girl. "I don't know, Mother," she said. "I suppose the child knows if the Alm-Uncle came himself."

Heidi looked at the woman and said firmly, "I know very well who wrapped me in the cover and brought me down in the sleigh. It was Grandfather."

"Then there must be something in what Peter said about the Alm-Uncle although we didn't believe him at the time," said the grand-mother. "Who could believe it possible! I didn't think the child would stay up there more than three weeks. How does she look, Brigitta?"

By this time Brigitta had carefully inspected Heidi from every angle so she was able to report: "She is as finely built as Adelheid was, but she has the dark eyes and curly hair of Tobias and the old man. I think she resembles both her parents."

During this time, Heidi's attention had not been idle. She had looked round carefully at everything in the room. Suddenly she said, "Look Grandmother! One of your shutters is loose. The grandfather would put a nail in and then the shutter would be all right. It will break the window-pane soon. See how it shakes!"

"Ah, my child," said the grandmother, "I can't

see but I can hear, and much more than the shutter banging. Everything in this house cracks and rattles as soon as the wind blows. It comes in from all sides. Everything seems to be loose. During the night, when the others are asleep, I often fear that the house is going to fall to pieces and kill us all. Alas, there is no one here to repair things. Peter doesn't know how to."

"But can't you see the shutter banging, Grandmother? Look! There it is, just over there!" said Heidi, pointing towards the shutter.

"Alas, child, I can see nothing, nothing!" lamented the grandmother.

"But if I go outside and open the shutter properly so that it is lighter, won't you see then, Grandmother?"

"No, not even then. Nobody can ever make it light for me."

"But if you go outside into the white snow then surely it will be light. Come with me, Grandmother, and I will show you." Heidi, beginning to feel very distressed, took the old woman's hand and tried to lead her.

"Just let me sit, child. It will always be dark for me."

"But surely in summer it will be different, Grandmother," comforted Heidi, becoming more and more anxious to help. "Surely then it will be light for you! When the sun shines on the mountains and on the flowers and turns them all to crimson and gold, then everything will be bright and wonderful for you."

"Ah, child, I shall never again see the flaming mountains nor the little golden flowers up there. It will never again be light for me on this earth, never!"

Suddenly, Heidi began to cry. Full of compassion she sobbed, "Who then can help you? Is there no one?"

The grandmother tried to comfort the child. The old woman was touched to hear her sob so bitterly. Heidi rarely cried, but when she did her grief was not easily overcome. At last the grandmother said, "Come, my dear Heidi, come and I will explain something to you. You see, when one can't see one likes to hear a kind word and I like to hear you talking. Come, sit here close to me and tell me what you have been doing up there and all about the grandfather. I knew him very well years ago. But for many years now I have only heard of him from Peter, and Peter doesn't talk much."

Suddenly, Heidi had a new idea. Quickly she wiped away her tears and said comfortingly, "You wait, Grandmother, and I shall tell Grandfather everything. He will make it light for you again and will repair the cottage for you. He can do everything."

The grandmother was silent now and Heidi began to give a lively account of her life, of summer days on the pasture and her present life in winter with the grandfather. She described the things he could make from wood—benches and chairs and beautiful mangers where the hay was put for Little Swan and Little Bear, and a big new tub for bathing in summer, a new milk bowl and a spoon. Heidi was quite carried away describing all the beautiful things which could be made from pieces of wood. The grandmother listened intently and every now and then she would say, "Do you hear, Brigitta? Do you hear what she says about the Alm-Uncle?"

Suddenly the story was interrupted by a loud clatter at the door and in tramped Peter. He stopped abruptly and gaped when he saw Heidi, but managed a friendly grin as she greeted him, "Good evening, Peter!"

"Is the boy back from school already?" asked the

grandmother in surprise. "An afternoon has not passed so quickly for me for a long time! "Good evening, Peter. How did you get on with your reading to-day?"

"Just as usual," answered Peter.

"Well, well," sighed the grandmother gently. "I thought there might perhaps be a change by this time, especially as you are going to be twelve years old in February."

"What do you mean by change, Grandmother?" Heidi asked with interest.

"I hoped he would be able to learn to read," explained the grand-mother. "Up there on the shelf is an old hymn book with beautiful hymns in it. I have not heard them for a very long time and I can't remember them now. So I had hoped if Peter could learn to read he would be able to read the hymns to me. But he can't learn the letters. It is too difficult for him."

"I think I had better light the lamp. It is getting quite dark," said Peter's mother, who was still busy patching his jacket. "This afternoon has flown by without my noticing."

Heidi jumped up from her chair, stretched out her hand quickly to the grandmother and said,

"Good-bye, Grandmother. I have to go home when it gets dark." She said good night to Peter and his mother and went towards the door. But the grandmother called anxiously, "Wait, wait, Heidi! You mustn't go alone. Peter will go with you. Do you hear? Take care of the child, Peter, and see that she doesn't fall down. And don't loiter on the way in case she catches cold, do you hear? Has she got a warm scarf?"

"I haven't got a scarf," replied Heidi, "but I shall not be cold."

With these words she was outside the house and away so quickly that Peter could hardly keep pace. "Run after her, Brigitta!" the grandmother called. The child will be frozen to death on such a night. Take my scarf! Hurry up now and run quickly!"

Brigitta obeyed. The children had only gone a little way up the mountain when they saw the grandfather coming down and soon he stood beside them.

"Good, Heidi! You have kept your word," he praised her. Then wrapping her snugly in the cover he picked her up and turned back up the mountain.

Brigitta saw the old man lift the child, well wrapped up, into his arms. She returned with Peter to the cottage and told the grandmother with amusement what she had seen.

The grandmother was both astonished and glad. "God be thanked that he is good to thy child! If only he would allow her to come again! She is a great comfort and what a kind heart she has!" Until the grandmother went to bed she kept repeating, "If only she could come again! Then I might have something to look forward to in this world! She has done me so much good. She has such a loving little heart and how good she is at telling her story."

Brigitta agreed with her mother, and Peter was well pleased, saying, "I told you so," with great satisfaction.

All the way, Heidi chatted to the grandfather although he could not make out a word of the muffled voice coming from inside the sack. So he said, "Wait until we get home, then you can tell me all about it."

As soon as they entered the hut and Heidi was released from her wrapping she said, "Grandfather, to-morrow we must take the hammer and plenty of long nails to fix the grandmother's shutters and all the loose boards because her house rattles and shakes all over!"

"Must we, indeed! And who told you so?" inquired the grandfather.

"Nobody told me but I know myself," replied Heidi, "for everything is loose and the grandmother cannot sleep if she is afraid that any minute the house will fall down on their heads. And for her everything is dark and she thinks that nobody can ever make it light for her again; but you can do it, Grandfather, I am sure. Think how sad it is for her always having to sit in the dark, and being frightened; and only you can help her. To-morrow we will go and help her, won't we, Grandfather?"

Heidi clung tightly to the grandfather and looked up at him with eagerness and confidence. For a little while the old man looked down at the child, then he said, "Yes, Heidi, we will go and see about the repairs. We can do that to-morrow."

The child started to skip round the room, chanting joyfully, "To-morrow we'll go! To-morrow we'll go!"

The grandfather kept his promise and on the following afternoon they took the same sleigh drive as they had done the previous day. Once again the old man set the child down before the door of Goat

Peter's cottage and said, "Go in now and come away again whenever it gets dark!"

Scarcely had Heidi opened the door and skipped into the room when the grandmother called from the corner, "It is Heidi! Here comes the child!" In her eagerness, she let the thread drop from her fingers and the wheel stood still as both her arms stretched out towards the child. Heidi ran to her at once, and drawing the little chair close to her she sat down at her side. Once again there was so much she had to tell the grandmother and so many questions she had to ask. But suddenly such heavy blows sounded against the wall that the grandmother started violently and nearly upset the spinning wheel. "Mercy on us!" she exclaimed, trembling. "What is that? The house must be falling about us!" Heidi grasped her arm firmly and comforted her, "No, no, Grandmother! Don't be afraid! It is only Grandfather hammering. He will fix everything so that you don't need to be afraid any more."

"Is it possible? Then the Lord has not forgotten us!" the grandmother exclaimed. "Did you hear that, Brigitta? If it is the Alm-Uncle, go and tell him to come in so that I can thank him!"

Brigitta went outside. The Alm-Uncle was busy
nailing some strong planks to the wall, knocking in
the nails with great vigour. Brigitta approached and
said, "Good evening, Uncle! Mother and I want to
thank you for your kindness and she would like to
tell you herself how grateful she is."

"That will do," interrupted the old man. "I know
what you think of the Alm-Uncle. Go back inside. I
can find out for myself what is needed here."

Brigitta obeyed at once for the Uncle expressed
himself in a way which brooked no opposition.

He knocked and hammered his way all round the
house and then climbed the narrow little stair up to
the roof, and hammered away there until he had
used his last nail. By the time he had finished, darkness had fallen and he had no sooner come down
and got out the sleigh from behind the shed than
Heidi appeared. As on the previous day, the grandfather wrapped her up and took her in his arms,
and, dragging the sleigh behind, made his way back
up the mountain. For although he had to drag the
heavy sleigh, he was afraid that if Heidi sat in it
alone, her wrappings would come loose and then
she would get very cold; so he carried her snug and
warm in his arms.

And so the winter passed. After many lonely years a great happiness had entered the joyless life of the old blind grandmother, and her days were no longer dreary and dark for now she had something to look forward to. From early morning she listened for Heidi's familiar tripping steps. The child became very attached to the old grandmother. And Heidi, sitting beside her, would chat so merrily that the grandmother hardly noticed the passing of time, and never bothered to ask Brigitta whether the day was over, as she used to do. Indeed, as Heidi left, the old lady would remark on how short the afternoon had been. She continually asked Brigitta to say if the child looked well and Brigitta always replied, "She looks the picture of health!" As soon as she understood that nobody, not even the grandfather, could help the old woman, Heidi was very sad; but the grandmother told her again and again that she felt the darkness much less when Heidi was with her. So every fine winter's day Heidi came down on the sleigh. Without any fuss, the grandfather always packed in his tools and he spent many afternoons repairing the cottage. All his good work soon had its effect and the cottage no longer rattled and groaned when the wind blew around it. The grandmother said she had not slept so well for many a year and that she would never forget what the Alm-Uncle had done for her.

CHAPTER 5

Two Visitors to the Alm-Hut

Quickly the winter passed, and more quickly still the happy days of summer; and now another winter was drawing to its close. Heidi was happy as a bird and each day she looked forward eagerly to the coming of spring when the warm south wind would sweep through the fir trees and across the valley, melting the last patch of snow on the lower slopes. Long days on the pasture would return and this seemed to Heidi the greatest joy of all. She was eight years old now and had learnt a great deal during the time she had lived with the Alm-Uncle. She knew how to manage the goats, and Little Swan and Little Bear would follow her about, bleating at the very sound of her voice.

Twice during this winter Peter had come from the school in Dorfli with a message from the teacher telling the Alm-Uncle that the child he had staying with him should go to school since she was over the age and should, indeed, have attended the previous winter. On both occasions, the Alm-Uncle had replied that he had no intention of sending the child to school.

When the sun had melted all the snow on the mountain, and the snowdrops were appearing and the fir trees had shaken off the weight of snow and were once again waving their green branches in the wind, Heidi ran back and forth with pleasure between the goat shed, the trees and the hut, to show her grandfather how big the area of green grass under the trees had grown. One sunny morning in March, as she ran out of the house, she was startled to come face to face with an old gentlemen dressed in black. He stood regarding her gravely for a time and then, thinking that his unexpected appearance had frightened her, he said kindly, "It is all right. You need not be afraid of me. You are Heidi, are you not? Where is your grandfather?"

"He is sitting at the table, making wooden spoons," replied Heidi and at once led him inside.

It was the old pastor from Dörfli who had known the uncle well in the old days. He walked towards the old man who was bent over his work, and addressed him.

"Good morning, neighbour!"

Astonished, the grandfather looked up, then rose, saying, "Good morning, pastor!" Offering his seat to the visitor, he added, "Pray sit down, if you do not mind a wooden seat."

The pastor seated himself. "I have not seen you for a long time, neighbour," he said.

"Nor I you!"

"I have come to-day to discuss something with you," continued the pastor. "I think perhaps you know what it is I want to talk to you about, and that I am anxious to hear what you intend to do about a certain matter."

There was a silence. The pastor glanced quickly towards the child, who stood by the door and watched the newcomer with interest.

"Heidi, go and see how the goats are getting along!" said the grandfather. "You may take them a little salt, and stay with them until I come!"

Heidi disappeared at once.

"The child should have gone to school a year

ago," said the pastor now. "The school master reminded you often but you ignored him. What is it you intend should become of the child, neighbour?"

"I intend that she should not go to school!"

The pastor looked with surprise at the old man who sat on his bench with his arms folded determinedly.

"But how is the child going to grow up?" asked the pastor reasonably.

"She will grow up with the goats and birds. That way she will learn nothing evil."

"But the child is neither a goat nor a bird but a human being," pleaded the pastor. "Though she learns nothing evil from her companions, they cannot teach her her A B Cs! Learn she must, and the time has come to begin. I came to speak a word to you in time, neighbour, so that you may think it over at your leisure and make arrangements during the summer. The child must not be allowed to run about another winter without taking lessons. Next winter he must attend school regularly!"

"No, she will not go, pastor!" muttered the old man with unwavering determination.

"Do you really think there is no way of making

you see reason if you insist so stubbornly on this decision?" asked the pastor, beginning to lose patience. "You have lived in the world and have seen and learnt a lot. I should have thought you would have had more sense, neighbour."

"You think so? asked the old man, and the tremor in his voice betrayed that he was no longer calm. "And do you really think that next winter I shall send a delicate child on a two hours' walk down the mountain on ice-cold mornings in storm and snow, and allow her to return at night when there may be a wind raging fit to blow a man over, let alone a child? Perhaps the pastor still remembers the child's mother, Adelheid. She was a sleep-walker and had a delicate constitution. Might not the health of this child, who is also finely built, be endangered by so much exertion? I wonder who can force me to send her? I shall take it to the highest law court in the country and then we shall see who can force me!"

"You are quite right, neighbour," agreed the pastor, amicably. "It would not be possible to send the child from here. But I see the child is dear to you. For her sake, do what you ought to have done long ago. Come down into Dörfli and live amongst us! What a life you live here, alone and embittered towards God and men. If anything should happen to you up here in the mountains who would come to your assistance? I cannot understand how you are not frozen to death in this hut of yours in the winter-time. How does this delicate child stand up to it?"

"I see to it that she is not cold, and that she has a good warm bed, I should like the pastor to know. And another thing: I get all the wood I need. If the pastor cares to look into my wood-shed he will soon see! There is plenty there! The fire is never out in my hut all through the winter. As for living down in the valley, it is out of the question. The people down there despise me and I them. For all our sakes, it is better we stay apart."

"No, no, you are quite wrong!" the pastor said warmly. "The people down below don't dislike you half as much as you think. Take my advice, neighbour! Make your peace with God, ask His forgiveness and then come and see how people will change towards you and how happy you will be!"

The pastor rose. He held out his hand to the old man and repeated with kindly emphasis, "I am counting on it, neighbour! Next winter you'll come back to live with us in the valley and we'll be good neighbours again, as we used to be. I would be disappointed to think that you were coming back only because of the school business. Promise me that you will live amongst us again, reconciled to God and man!"

The Alm-Uncle shook hands with the pastor but insisted firmly, "I know you mean well, but as to what you expect me to do—no! Once and for all I tell you I will not send the child, nor will I come down to live in the valley."

"Then God help you!" sighed the pastor and sadly made his way back down the mountain to the village.

As a result of the interview, the Alm-Uncle was in a very black mood, and when Heidi asked in the afternoon, "Shall we go down to the grandmother's now?" he replied harshly, "Not to-day!" He was silent the whole day and the following morning, when Heidi asked again, "Shall we go to-day to see the grandmother?" he turned away abruptly, mumbling, "Perhaps."

But before the dinner dishes had been cleared away another visitor had arrived. It was cousin Dete, dressed in a beautiful gown which swept the

floor and wearing on her head a very fine hat with
feathers. The Alm-Uncle examined her from head
to foot in amazement. But Dete was all prepared to
make friendly conversation and at once adopted a
flattering tone.

"How well the child looks! I hardly recognised
her! I can see that she has not had a bad time with
the Alm-Uncle, far from it! I have often thought of
taking the child back for I can imagine that she is in
your way. Day and night I have thought about what
to do with her and that's why I am here to-day. I
have just heard of something that would be a piece
of luck for Heidi. I have fixed everything. It is really
a wonderful chance. The people I am in service with
have some very wealthy relations. They live in the
most beautiful house in Frankfurt and they have an
only daughter who is an invalid and has to be
wheeled in a chair. She is very much alone and has
her lessons with a private teacher, which, of course,
is very boring for her. Now she would like a playmate so her people have asked my mistress to help
them find a companion. The lady house-keeper
thinks that a simple, unspoilt child, one different
from the children now-a-days, would be most suitable. Naturally I thought of Heidi and went at once

to the lady and told her all about our child's character. She agreed immediately to take her. No one can foresee what good fortune will be in store for Heidi. If the people become fond of her and if something should happen to their own little daughter—and who knows when she is so weak—then in all likelihood they would not want to be without a child— then it would be the most unheard-of luck—"

"Do you think you have just about finished?" interrupted the Alm-Uncle who had held his peace up till now.

"Ugh!" exclaimed Dete, tossing her head. "You behave as though I were telling you something of no consequence. Anybody in Prattigau would thank God if I were to bring such news!"

"You may take your news where you like. I want to hear no more of it," replied the Uncle dryly.

This threw Dete immediately into a passion. "Well!" she stormed, "if that is all you have to say, Uncle, I will speak my mind, too. The child is eight years old now, but she knows nothing. You neither want her to attend school nor to go to church. Oh, I have heard all about it in Dörfli. She is my sister's child and I am responsible for what happens to her. When such a good chance comes her way only one who cared nothing for her welfare would oppose it. But I tell you, I won't give in and people are on my side. There is not a single person who would not take my part—and they are all against you. And if you are thinking of taking it to law, think well, Uncle! There are things that could be brought up against you which you wouldn't like to hear."

"Hold your tongue!" thundered the uncle, his eyes ablaze with anger. "Very well, then. Take the child away and ruin her! And never let me set eyes on you again, with that ridiculous hat on your head and such words on your tongue!" Then the uncle turned from her abruptly and strode from the hut.

"You have made Grandfather angry," said Heidi, fixing dark, smouldering eyes on her aunt.

"Oh, he'll soon get over it," replied Dete impatiently. "Come along now! Where are your clothes?"

"I won't go!" said Heidi defiantly.

"What did you say?" asked the aunt, about to fly into a temper. Then she softened her tone a little and continued more persuasively, "Come, come! You don't know any better. You have no idea how well off you will be." Then, going to the wardrobe, she took out Heidi's things and parcelled them together. "Come now! Here is your hat! What a sight it is! But never mind! It will do for to-day. Put it on, quickly."

"I am going to stay here," repeated Heidi.

"Don't be so silly. You are as obstinate as a goat. I suppose that is what you have learnt from them. But you've got to understand, the grandfather is cross and doesn't want to see us again, you heard him say so. He wants you to go with me, so now you mustn't make him more angry. You have no idea how nice it is in Frankfurt. But, of course, if you don't like it you can always come back here. By that time the grandfather will have recovered himself."

"Can I come straight home again tonight if I want to?" asked Heidi.

"Come along now and don't be silly! I said you can go home when you like. To-day we are only going as far as Mayenfeld but tomorrow we will travel by train, and the train can carry you home again as fast as the wind."

Aunt Dete took the bundle of clothes under one arm, grasped Heidi firmly by the other hand, and together they started to climb down the hill. It was still too early in the spring to take the goats up to the pasture, so Peter was still going to school in

Dörfli, but once in a while he took a day's holiday, for learning to read seemed not nearly as attractive a proposition as wandering about looking for thick sticks which might come in useful.

As Dete and Heidi approached the grandmother's hut, Peter appeared from round a corner of the cottage. He was carrying a huge bundle of thick hazel twigs, when the two figures approached. He stopped to stare at them as they passed by; then he called out after them, "Where are you going?"

"I have to go at once to Frankfurt with Aunt," answered Heidi, "but I am going to say good-bye to the grandmother first. She will be waiting for me and I must see her before I go."

"No, no," interrupted the aunt quickly. "It is much too late. You can see her next time you come back. Come along, now!" And she pulled the child along, afraid that she might again take it into her head to stay and that the grandmother would support her wishes.

Peter dashed into the cottage and dropped his bundle of sticks so noisily that the grandmother started up from her spinning, exclaiming fretfully, "What is it now? What is it?" And Peter's mother, who had been sitting by the table, said in her patient way, "What is it, Peter? What is the matter?"

"She is taking Heidi away!" gasped Peter.

"Who?" asked the grandmother in distress. "Taking her where, Peter?" But she soon guessed what had taken place, for her daughter had told her not long ago that she had seen Dete going up to the Alm-Uncle's. The old woman unfastened the window with trembling fingers and called out imploringly, "Dete, Dete, don't take the child away from us! Don't take Heidi away!"

Dete and Heidi heard the voice. Dete had evidently made out the grandmother's words for she grasped the child's hand still more firmly and ran as fast as she could.

Heidi, struggling to get her hand free, cried, "The grandmother is calling! I want to go to her!"

But that was exactly what the aunt did not want. She tried to soothe the child.

"Come quickly now or it will be too late and we will not be able to continue our journey to-morrow. You will soon see how much you will like Frankfurt. Perhaps you will never want to come back again. But if you do it will be quite simple. You could even take something home for the grandmother—something she would like."

This appealed to Heidi and she stopped trying to resist and started to run, too.

After a little while she asked, "What could I get for Grandmother?"

"Something nice," said the aunt. "Perhaps some nice soft rolls. She would enjoy that. It would be such a change from the dark bread."

"Oh, yes! She always gives it to Peter and says 'It is too hard for me.' I have heard her myself", admitted Heidi. "Let us hurry, then, Aunt Dete! We may reach Frankfurt to-day and I shall soon be back with the rolls." And Heidi started to run so fast that the aunt with her bundle could hardly keep pace with her. But she was glad to be having no more

difficulty with the child for now they had almost
reached the first houses in Dörfli and a lot of talk
and questions might have made Heidi change her
mind again. So Dete strode straight ahead holding
Heidi's hand tightly so that every one would see
that she had to hurry along because of the child. To
every question she merely answered, "I can't stop
now. We have a long way to go."

"Are you going away?" "Is she fleeing from the
Alm-Uncle?" "It's amazing that she has survived!"
"But how healthy she looks!" Questions and excla-
mations came from all sides and Dete was glad that
she didn't have to stop and that Heidi didn't say a
word but hurried on eagerly.

From that day on the Alm-Uncle looked even
more fierce and terrifying when he came down to
Dörfli. He spoke to no one and looked more threatening with his cheese-basket on his back and his
mountain stick in his hand. The old man ignored
everyone as he strode through the village to the
valley where he sold cheese and bought bread and
meat. After he had gone, the villagers stood around
watching   his   retreating   back   and   everyone
commented on his wild appearance and his total
lack of response to anyone's greeting.

They all agreed that it was a good thing that the child had been taken from him—they had noticed how Heidi hurried along as though afraid that her grandfather might catch them up. Everybody was of the same opinion; that it was a great blessing that the child had been taken away. Only the blind grandmother took the old man's part. When people came to the house to give her some spinning to do, she would tell them again and again how kind and good he had been to the child and what he had done for herself and her daughter; how he had spent many afternoons repairing the cottage which, without his help, would undoubtedly have collapsed upon them. This story soon got about in Dörfli, but most people thought the grandmother was too old to understand and too blind and hard of hearing to know exactly what went on around her.

It was as well it had been repaired, for the Alm-Uncle never came to Goat Peter's cottage now and the grandmother's days were once more passed in sighing and fretting. "Alas, all the joy and happiness has gone with the child!" she would say, "and the days are long and dreary! If only I might see Heidi again before I die!"

CHAPTER 6

A New Start For Heidi

In the house in Frankfurt, the little daughter of Herr Sesemann sat in the comfortable invalid chair in which all her life was spent and in which she had to be wheeled from room to room. Now she was in the room which they called the study, and where she had her lessons.

Clara's little face was pale and thin and her soft, gentle blue eyes were fixed at this moment on the door. To-day, time seemed to pass very slowly for her, for she was saying rather impatiently, "But isn't it time yet, Fräulein Rottenmeier?"

The lady thus addressed sat very upright at a small work-table and nodded. Principally because of her rather odd and very severe style of dress, Fräulein Rottenmeier presented an awe-inspiring appearance. Over her shoulders she wore a cape with a stiff collar and on her head a very elaborate cap. Since the death of Frau Sesemann, several years ago, Fräulein Rottenmeier had acted as house-keeper and manager of the domestic staff. Herr Sesemann very often went off on business trips, leaving Fräulein Rottenmeier in sole charge of the house, stipulating only that no decisions should be taken without first consulting his little daughter and that nothing should be done against her wish.

Just as Clara was asking the same question a second time, Dete and Heidi arrived at the door. Dete asked the coachman, who had descended from his box, whether it was too late to see Fräulein Rottenmeier.

"That's nothing to do with me," he muttered. "Ring the bell you'll find in the hall and Sebastian will come."

Dete rang the bell and the butler came down the stairs, the big round buttons of his livery in keeping with his round eyes which stared blankly at the two strangers.

"I wonder if it is too late to see Fräulein Rottenmeier?" Dete asked.

Sebastian stared frostily for a moment, then pressed a bell and disappeared without a word. Next a maid appeared. A spotless white cap was perched on top of her head. Regarding the visitors haughtily from the top of the stairs, "What is it?" she asked.

Dete repeated her request. Tinette disappeared, but very soon came back and called from above, "Come this way! You are expected."

Dete and Heidi went upstairs and followed Tinette into the study. At the door Dete stopped politely, still holding Heidi's hand firmly for there was no knowing what the child might do in strange surroundings.

Fräulein Rottenmeier rose slowly and came forward to examine the new playmate for the daughter of the house. She did not appear to be very pleased with what she saw. Heidi wore her simple little cotton dress and on her head, her old, crushed, straw hat. She gazed innocently from underneath it, staring with unconcealed surprise at the lady's towering headgear.

"What is your name?" asked Fräulein Rottenmeier, after a lengthy inspection of the child, who had returned her gaze steadily and inquiringly throughout.

"Heidi," the child answered distinctly.

"What? That is not a Christian name! You were surely not baptised so! What name were you given when you were christened?"

"I can't remember now," replied Heidi.

"What a foolish answer!" exclaimed the lady, shaking her head disapprovingly. "Dete, is the child stupid or impertinent?"

"I am so sorry! Would you kindly allow me to speak for the child? She is not accustomed to strangers," said Dete hastily, secretly nudging Heidi for having given such an unsuitable answer. "She certainly is not stupid, nor impertinent. It is

just that she always says exactly what she is thinking. This is the first time she has ever been in an
upper-class house and she knows nothing about
good manners. She is docile and willing to learn if
madam will have the patience. She was christened
Adelheid for her mother, my late sister."

"Well, at least that's a name one can pronounce,"
remarked Fräulein Rottenmeier. "But Dete, I must
say that for her age the child looks to me a little
strange. I told you that a companion for Fräulein
Clara had to be of her age to be able to share her
lessons and everything. Fräulein Clara is twelve
now. What is the age of the child?"

"With your permission," began Dete elaborately,
"I am not quite sure myself but I think she is a little
younger, but not much. She will be ten, or perhaps
a little more."

"I am eight now, the grandfather said," declared
Heidi. The aunt gave her another push but Heidi
was not in the least embarrassed.

"What! Only eight years old!" cried Fräulein
Rottenmeier indignantly. "Four years younger!
What use is that? And what have you learnt? Which
books did you use for your lessons?"

"None," replied Heidi.

"What? How did you learn to read?"

"I never learnt. Neither did Peter," said Heidi.

"Mercy! You cannot read! Is that true that you cannot read?" demanded Fräulein Rottenmeier, deeply shocked. What did you learn, then?"

"Nothing," said Heidi.

"Dete!" cried Fräulein Rottenmeier when she had recovered from this shock. "This is not the agreement at all! How dare you bring this child to me!"

But Dete was not easily frightened and replied boldly, "With madam's permission, the child is just what I understood madam wanted. Madam told me she wanted a companion unlike ordinary children. Therefore I chose this one because the older ones are not so unspoilt. But now I am afraid I must go. My mistress will be expecting me. If I may, I shall come again soon to see how the child is getting on."

With a curtsy, Dete left the room and quickly ran downstairs. For a moment Fräulein Rottenmeier was too surprised to speak, then she ran after Dete. There were many things which must be discussed if the child were to stay and the aunt seemed determined that she should.

Heidi still stood by the door where she had

remained since she entered the room. So far Clara had watched silently; now she beckoned to Heidi to come nearer.

Heidi went up to her.

"Would you rather be called Heidi or Adelheid?" asked Clara.

"I am always called Heidi," Heidi replied.

"Then I shall always call you that, too," said Clara "I like the name although never before have I heard it or seen a little girl like you. Has your hair always been short and curly like that?"

"Yes, I think so," replied Heidi.

"Did you come to Frankfurt yesterday, and are you pleased to be here?" Clara continued to ask.

"No, we came to-day. But to-morrow I am going home again with some white rolls for the grandmother."

"How strange you are!" Clara burst out. "You have been brought here to stay with me and share my lessons with me. What fun it will be now because you can't read at all. At least it will be a change. It is usually very dull and the mornings are so long! You see, every morning at ten my tutor comes and the lessons go on till two. That is far too long! Sometimes the tutor holds his book close to

his face as if he had suddenly become short-sighted
but I know quite well it is only because he is yawning; and Fräulein Rottenmeier takes out her handkerchief and holds it to her face as if she were
affected by what we are reading, but she too only
wants to yawn. But I don't dare, because if I only
did it once Fräulein Rottenmeier would fetch the
cot liver oil and say I was getting weak again, and
the worst thing of all is to take cod liver oil. But it
will be much more fun now. I can listen to you
learning to read."

Heidi shook her head doubtfully at the mention
of her learning to read.

"Of course, Heidi, you have to learn to read.
Everybody has to learn to read and my tutor is very
kind. He is never cross and he will explain everything to you. But nevertheless, you won't be able to
understand what he explains. Don't ask any questions, as you will only encourage him to continue
explaining and you'll understand even less. The
best thing to do is to wait until you've learnt more
and know about everything on your own, then what
he says will have some sort of meaning."

Just then Fräulein Rottenmeier came back into
the room. She had not succeeded in calling Dete

back and was apparently very annoyed about it. She had wanted at least to persuade Dete that Heidi was totally unsuitable to be Clara's companion and to complain at Dete's misleading behaviour. She felt even more annoyed at the thought that she herself had brought the problem on to her own head by agreeing to Heidi being fetched.

What was she going to do about it? She ran to and fro in a bother from the dining room to the study, and then began scolding Sebastian, who was studying the table he had just laid, to make sure nothing had been missed out.

"You can carry on day-dreaming tomorrow morning," she said crossly, "hurry up or we'll get no dinner today."

Then she bustled out, calling Tinette, but in such an irritable voice that the maid came up with even more of a swagger than usual. She looked so pert that Fräulein Rottenmeier did not dare scold her.

"See that a room is made ready for the child who has just arrived," she said, tight-lipped. "It's all ready; it just needs a duster over it." Sebastian had opened the folding doors of the study and quietly wheeled Clara into the other room. While he adjusted the chair Heidi placed herself before him and stared steadily up at him.

"Well, what is it you are looking at? he grumbled.

When Fräulein Rottenmeier returned she was just in time to hear Heidi say, "You look like Peter."

She raised her hands in horror. "Really!" she murmured. "She treats the butler as an equal! The child knows absolutely nothing!"

Sebastian helped Clara to her seat at the table and Fräulein Rottenmeier seated herself beside her, motioning Heidi to sit opposite. Beside Heidi's plate lay a lovely white roll. She glanced at it happily. The resemblance Heidi had discovered in Sebastian seemed to have given her confidence in him for she sat as quiet as a mouse until he came to her side to serve the fish, then she pointed to the roll and asked, "May I have it?"

Sebastian nodded, glancing sideways at Fräulein Rottenmeier to see what effect the question had had on her.

Immediately Heidi took the roll and put it into her pocket. Sebastian hid a smile. Motionless and silent, he stood at her side, waiting for her to take her helping of fish for it was not his place to speak

or move away until Heidi had helped herself. For a
few seconds Heidi looked at him wonderingly, then
she asked, "May I have a little of that, too?"
Sebastian nodded again. "Then give me some,
please," she said, looking calmly at her plate. At this
breach of etiquette Sebastian was almost in danger
of losing control of his features and the arm which
held the dish was beginning to shake.

"You can leave the dish on the table and come
back afterwards," ordered Fräulein Rottenmeier,
looking very severe, and Sebastian disappeared at
once.

"Adelheid, I see I shall have to teach you the first
simple rules of good behaviour," said the lady with
a deep sigh. "First of all I will show you how to
behave at the table and improve your manners."

She instructed Heidi thoroughly and clearly on
what she had to do. "Then," she went on to
explain, "I must impress upon you particularly that
you are not to speak to Sebastian at table unless the
question or remark is absolutely necessary, and
even then you must not address him as a friend. Do
you understand? And so with Tinette. You will
address *me* as you hear others do. Clara will decide
for herself what you are to call her."

"Clara, of course!" Clara interrupted.

Then followed a long list of rules about getting up and going to bed, about entering and leaving a room, about being tidy and shutting doors. All of a sudden Heidi's eyes closed, for she had been up since five o'clock that morning and had had a long journey. She leaned back in her chair, fast asleep. When Fräulein Rottenmeier had finished her lecture at last, she said, "Now, remember everything I have said, Adelheid! Have you understood it all?"

"Heidi has been asleep for ever so long," Clara said with amusement. She had not had such an entertaining dinner for a long time!

"It is really shocking how much trouble this child is causing," exclaimed Fräulein Rottenmeier angrily and rang the bell so violently that both Sebastian and Tinette came rushing in. But in spite of all the noise Heidi slept on and it was only with great difficulty that they succeeded in awakening her so that she could be shown to her bedroom which was at the end of a long passage, beyond those of Clara and Fräulein Rottenmeier.

CHAPTER 7

An Eventful Day

Heidi awoke in the morning and looked around in bewilderment. She blinked and rubbed her eyes but it did not help her to remember where she was. She was lying in a high white bed in a big room and daylight streamed in between long white curtains. There were two arm-chairs covered in a floral material. A sofa stood against the wall with a round table in front of it and in the corner there was a wash-stand with all sorts of objects on it which were entirely new to Heidi.

Suddenly she remembered that she was in Frankfurt and the events of the previous day came back to her quite clearly. She remembered the long list of instructions given to her by Fräulein Rottenmeier, up to the point at which she must

have fallen asleep. Heidi jumped out of bed and
dressed; then went from one window to the other to
try to get a glimpse of the sky and the countryside
outside. Behind the big curtains she felt like a bird
in a cage. As she could not manage to pull them
aside she crept underneath to get to the window. It
was so high that she could only just see over the sill.
However, the view was not one of pleasant green
fields but only of walls and windows. She ran backwards and forwards from one window to another,
but the view was just the same. It frightened her to
think that she could not see the sky, for she was
used to rising early and running outside straight
away to inspect the meadows, the blue sky, the sun
and the trees and flowers. Heidi couldn't believe
that there might be no green grass or snow on the
mountain slopes. She was like a captive bird, trying
to fly out into the free air through the bars of its
cage. But the windows would not open, and her
little fingers were not strong enough to prise them
open from the bottom. At last she realised that her
efforts were in vain, and she started to consider
going outside and round the house until she found
the grass. Then she remembered that the previous
night when she arrived, she had seen only hard

pavements in front of the house. Presently there came a knock at the door and Tinette popped her head round, saying in a bored voice, "Breakfast is ready!"

Heidi failed to understand that this was an invitation, for the sour expression on Tinette's face had suggested rather a warning to stay away. So it seemed to Heidi, at any rate, and she acted accordingly. She took the little stool from under the table, put it in a corner, sat down and waited quietly to see what would happen next. After some time Fräulein Rottenmeier bustled along with a great deal of noise. Once again she seemed to be thoroughly annoyed and shouted at Heidi, "What is the matter with you, Adelheid? Don't you know what breakfast is? Come along!"

This Heidi understood and followed at once. Clara had been seated in the dining-room for some time and she greeted Heidi in a friendly way. Her face wore a much happier expression than usual for she was looking forward to all kinds of unexpected events that day. Breakfast passed without incident. Heidi ate her rolls very nicely and when they had finished Clara was wheeled back to the study. Fräulein Rottenmeier told Heidi to follow and remain with Clara until the tutor arrived to begin lessons. As soon as the children were alone together Heidi asked, "How can I see right down to the ground?"

"You just open the window and look out!" replied Clara, amused.

"But the windows won't open," replied Heidi sadly.

"Oh yes," Clara assured her, "but you can't do it alone. Neither can I. But if you see Sebastian he will open them for you."

Heidi sighed with relief, for the house had begun to make her feel as though she were a prisoner. Then Clara began to ask Heidi about her home and Heidi was delighted to tell her all about the Alm and the goats and the pasture and everything that was dear to her.

In the meantime the tutor had arrived, but Fräulein Rottenmeier did not show him into the study as usual. She wanted to talk to him first and led him to the dining-room. There, in great agitation, she began to describe to him the awkward situation which had arisen and told him how, some time ago, she had persuaded Herr Sesemann to get a companion for Clara as it would help Clara at her lessons and give her some amusement during her leisure hours. In actual fact, Fräulein Rottenmeier had wanted this for her own benefit, as it would no longer necessitate her own continual attendance on the sick child. The father had replied that he was delighted for his daughter to have a companion, as long as she was given exactly the same kindness and care as Clara, for he would not tolerate any tormenting of the child—"a quite unnecessary and tactless remark," added Fräulein Rottenmeier. She recounted how dreadfully she had been deceived and she went on to enlighten the tutor on all the dreadful things of which Heidi had so far been found guilty, and how, in view of Heidi's complete ignorance, the tutor would have to begin at the very beginning with the A B C, and how she herself had had to give the child instruction on the simplest rules of behaviour. There was only one way out of the situation, in Fräulein Rottenmeier's opinion, and that was for the tutor to insist that it was impossible to teach two children so far apart in age without retarding-Clara's progress. That would be a very good reason for Herr Sesemann's sending the child back home. Herr Sesemann knew the child had arrived and without his consent

Fräulein Rottenmeier could not send her away again.

However, the tutor was cautious and unwilling to commit himself. With many words of comfort he assured Fräulein Rottenmeier that though the child were backward in some things she might be quite advanced in other respects and that regular lessons might very well restore the balance. When Fräulein Rottenmeier at last realised that she would get very little support from the tutor she opened the door to the study and allowed him him to go through to the children. She paced up and down the dining room, silently pondering how the servants should be instructed to address Adelheid. The father had expressly stated that she was to be treated exactly like his own daughter, and this would probably refer particularly to her dealings with the servants. However, her musing was suddenly interrupted, for before many minutes had passed, a dreadful noise came from the study. Then there was a loud cry from Sebastian. Fräulein Rottenmeier rushed in to find the whole room in complete disorder; books, copy-books, ink-stand; and across the table, on to the floor and across the carpet there flowed a stream of ink. Heidi was nowhere to be seen.

"What is all this?" cried Fräulein Rottenmeier. "Carpet, books, work basket, everything covered with ink! I never saw such a mess! I have no doubt that wretched child is to blame!"

The tutor looked very distressed but Clara was following events with obvious amusement.

"Yes, Heidi did it, but not on purpose. She mustn't be punished. It was just that she was in such a hurry to get away that she tugged the table-cloth and then everything fell on the floor. She wanted to see the carriages passing; that's why she rushed out. Perhaps she has never seen one before!"

"What did I tell you? The creature doesn't know the first thing! She has no idea what a lesson is— that she must sit still and listen. But where is the little trouble-maker? Surely she hasn't run away! Whatever will Herr Sesemann say?"

Fräulein Rottenmeier ran downstairs. There stood Heidi in the open doorway looking out into the street in complete bewilderment.

"What is the matter? What are you thinking of to run away like that?" Fräulein Rottenmeier shouted at the child.

"I thought I heard the fir trees rustling but I can't find them and I don't hear them any more," said

Heidi disconsolately, turning her head in the direction of the disappearing carriages. The rumbling of their wheels had seemed to her like the howling of the wind in the fir trees at home and she had tried to follow the sound.

"Fir trees! What nonsense! Do you think we live in a wood! Come and see the mess you have made!"

Heidi followed Fräulein Rottenmeier upstairs. She gazed in astonishment at the havoc she had created, for in her haste to get downstairs she had noticed nothing.

"You won't do this a second time," warned Fräulein Rottenmeier. "During lessons you will sit still and pay attention! And if you can't do that I will have to tie you to your chair. Do you understand?"

"Yes," said Heidi. "I shall be good now."

Sebastian and Tinette were called in to restore order and the tutor went away because there could be no more lessons that day— there had not even been time for yawning!

Clara always rested in the afternoons, so Heidi was told she might do as she pleased. This suited her perfectly because there was something she very much wanted to do. But she needed assistance, and for this reason she posted herself in front of the dining-room door, right in the centre of the hall so that she would not miss the person to whom she wished to speak. It was not very long before Sebastian came upstairs carrying a large tray. Heidi addressed him formally, as Fräulein Rottenmeier had instructed her.

"Is there something the little fräulein wants?" inquired Sebastian, carrying the silver into the dining-room. "I only wanted to ask you something—but nothing nasty like this morning," said Heidi, hastily, eager to placate him, for Sebastian appeared to be in a bad mood, and Heidi was sure that it was because she had spilt ink on the floor.

"Oh yes, and why are you talking to me in that manner?" replied Sebastian, in an offended tone, obviously still cross.

"Fräulein Rottenmeier ordered me always to speak to you like that," said Heidi.

Sebastian laughed, to Heidi's astonishment, and added in a friendly way, "What is it that the little fräulein wants?"

"My name is Heidi, not fräulein," replied Heidi, now put out herself.

"Exactly, but the lady in question has ordered me
to call you fräulein," he explained.

"Oh, well, I had better accept it," said Heidi
quietly, for she had realised that whatever
Fräulein Rottenmeier said was to be obeyed
absolutely. "So now I have three names," she
sighed.

"What was it the little fräulein wanted to ask?"
said Sebastian kindly as he went through to the
dining room to put away the cutlery.

"How do you open a window, Sebastian?"

"Like this!" And he opened one of the large
windows in the dining-room.

Heidi crossed over to the window but she was not
tall enough to be able to see out.

"Here you are!" said Sebastian, bringing a high
stool. "Now the little fräulein can see everything
that is going on in the street down below."

Cheerfully Heidi climbed up and at last managed
to see out of the window. Greatly disappointed, she
withdrew her head almost at once. "But I can only
see the stony street! Nothing else!" she said sadly.
"If you go round the house what do you see on the
other side, Sebastian?"

"Just the same!" he replied.

"But where have you to go to see over the whole valley?" she asked.

"Then you must climb a high tower or a church steeple, like that one with the golden ball. From there you can see ever so far."

At that, Heidi quickly jumped down from her stool and raced downstairs into the street. But it was not so easy as she had imagined. When she saw the steeple from the window it looked as though she only had to cross the street to reach it. But although she had walked right down the street she had not come to the steeple and she could not even see it any longer. She walked on and on. Many people passed but they all seemed to be in such a hurry that Heidi did not like to stop any of them to ask the way. Then Heidi saw a boy standing on the street corner with a barrel organ and, perched on his arm, a very strange-looking little animal. Heidi went forward and asked, "Where is the tower with the golden ball on the top?"

"Don't know!" answered the boy.

"Who can tell me, then?" asked Heidi again.

"Don't know."

"Don't you know of any church with a high steeple?"

"Yes, I know one!"

"Well, then, come and show it to me!"

"You show me first what you will give me for it!" said the boy, holding his hand out. Heidi searched in her pocket and found a pretty little card on which was printed a wreath of red roses. It was not easy to part with it for it had been given to her by Clara only that morning. But she longed to be able to look down over the green slopes into the valley. "There," said Heidi, "would you like this?"

The boy withdrew his hand and shook his head.

"What do you want, then?" asked Heidi, cheerfully putting away her little picture.

"Money," said the boy.

"I haven't got any now, but Clara will give me some later. How much do you want?"

"Twopence."

"Well, come along, then!"

They walked down a long street and on the way Heidi asked her companion what he was carrying on his back. He told her it was a barrel organ which played beautiful music when you turned the handle. All at once they found themselves in front of an old church with a high steeple. The boy stood still and pointed at it.

"But how can I get in?" asked Heidi when she saw that the doors were closed.

"Don't know," came the reply.

"Perhaps I could ring the bell as we do for Sebastian." Heidi had discovered a bell in the wall which she now pulled as hard as she could.

"When I go up you must wait here for me for I don't know my way back and you must show it to me."

"What will I get for it?"

"What do you want?"

"Another twopence."

They heard steps inside and the door creaked open. An old man appeared, looking first surprised and then angry when he saw the children. "How dare you ring the bell like that!" he shouted at them. "Can't you read the notice? 'Visitors wishing to go to the top of the tower, please ring!' "

The boy said nothing but pointed to Heidi.

"But that's just what I want!" said Heidi.

"Why do you want to go up there?" asked the caretaker. "Did somebody send you?"

"No," said Heidi. "I would just like to go up to the top and look down."

"Be off with you! And don't dare to try this trick

on me again!" said the old man and was about to
close the door; but Heidi grasped his coat and cried
beseechingly, "Let me go up just once!"

The imploring look in Heidi's eyes made the old
man change his mind. He took her hand and said
kindly, "If you really want it so much I will take you
up."

The boy sat down on the stone steps and
prepared to wait.

Together Heidi and the old man climbed many,
many steps which became smaller and smaller as
they went up, until at last, a very narrow little stair
led up to the top of the tower. The caretaker lifted
Heidi up to let her see out of the window. "Now
you can look down," he said.

Heidi saw nothing but roofs, steeples and chim-
neys. She withdrew her head presently and said,
very dispiritedly, "It is not at all as I expected."

"There! You see how a little one like you knows
nothing about views. Now come down and never
ring my bell again!"

The old man put Heidi back down on the floor
and went ahead of her down the narrow stair. When
the steps got broader they came to the caretaker's
little room and beside it, underneath the sloping

roof, stood a big basket. In front of it sat a big grey
cat which snarled and spat because inside the
basket lived her family and she wanted to warn
everybody not to meddle with them. Heidi looked
at her in amazement. She had never seen such a big
cat. There were scores of mice in the old tower and
the cat had no difficulty in catching half a dozen
every day, for her kittens. The caretaker saw the
look of delight on Heidi's face and said, "Come!
She won't hurt you when I am here. You can still
look at the kittens."

Heidi went over to the basket and exclaimed
joyfully, "Oh, what sweet little kittens!"

"Would you like one?" asked the old man as he
watched Heidi with amusement.

"For myself? To keep?" whispered Heidi, who
could hardly believe her luck.

"Yes, you can have them all if you like," he said,
thinking this would be a better way of getting rid of
them than drowning.

Heidi was overjoyed. There was certainly plenty
of room in the big house and how happy the kittens
would make Clara!

"But how can I carry them away?" asked Heidi,
picking some of them up, but the big cat sprang at

her arm and hissed at her so fiercely that she shrank
back.

"I will bring them if you tell me the address," said
the old man.

"Herr Sesemann's. On the door there is a dog's
head with a gold ring in its mouth."

The caretaker did not need such a detailed
description. He had been in the church for many
years and knew every house in the district.

"I know the house."

"If only I could take one or two with me—one for
me and one for Clara! May I?"

"Yes! Take them."

Heidi's eyes shone with delight. She chose a
white one and a tabby and put one into her right
and one into her left pocket. Then they went downstairs.

The boy was still sitting on the steps outside. He
jumped up when he saw Heidi but it took Heidi
several minutes of detailed description of the house
and its surroundings before the boy realised where
she had to go and they then quickly reached the
house. Heidi rang the bell and Sebastian opened
the door. When he saw Heidi he hustled her inside.

"Quickly! Into the dining-room! They are all at

table and Fräulein Rottenmeier looks like a loaded cannon. But why did you run away like that?"

Heidi went into the room. Fräulein Rottenmeier did not look up, Clara said nothing and it was an altogether uneasy atmosphere. When Heidi was seated Fräulein Rottenmeier began in a very severe and solemn voice:

"Adelheid! I shall talk to you afterwards. I will only say now that you have behaved exceedingly badly, leaving the house without permission and wandering about the streets until such a late hour without telling anyone. Your conduct is unparalleled!"

"Miaow!" It sounded like an answer.

Now the lady's temper rose, "What Adelheid! You are rude as well as naughty! I warn you!"

"I didn't—," began Heidi. "Miaow! Miaow!"

Sebastian could conceal his amusement no longer and had to leave the room.

"That will do!" Fräulein Rottenmeier tried to say, but her voice cracked with excitement. "Get up and leave the room!"

Heidi, frightened, got up and tried to explain, "I really didn't— Miaow! Miaow!"

"But Heidi," Clara said reproachfully, "when

you see it makes Fräulein Rottenmeier angry why
do you go on saying 'Miaow'?"

"I didn't. It is the kittens!"

"What! Cats!" screamed Fräulein Rottenmeier.
"Sebastian! Tinette! Find the horrid animals!
Remove them at once!"

The lady rushed into the study and locked the
door for she disliked cats more than anything.

Sebastian had to wait outside the door until his
face was straight again. When he had served Heidi
he had noticed the little kitten's head peeping out of
her pocket and had guessed what would happen.
When at last he entered the room everything
seemed quiet and peaceful again. Clara had the
kittens on her lap and Heidi knelt beside her. Both
played happily with the two tiny animals.

"Sebastian," said Clara. "You must help us to
find a place for the kittens where Fräulein
Rottenmeier will not find them, because she is
afraid of them and wants to get rid of them. Where
can we put them?"

"I shall see to that, Fräulein Clara," replied
Sebastian willingly. "I shall prepare a nice bed in a
basket and put it in a place where madam is not
likely to go; rely on me!" He made ready at once,

chuckling to himself, for he realised that there would be a further to-do about this at some time in the future, and Sebastian was by no means unhappy at the thought of Fräulein Rottenmeier being unsettled.

Much later Fräulein Rottenmeier opened the door an inch or two and called through the slit, "Are the horrid animals away?"

"Yes! Yes!" answered Sebastian, quietly collecting the kittens from Clara's lap and disappearing with them.

The lecture for Heidi was put off until the following day as Fräulein Rottenmeier felt too exhausted, after her ordeal of irritation, anger and fear, through which the innocent Heidi had put her, so she retired quietly. Clara and Heidi went cheerfully to bed, knowing that the kittens were all right.

CHAPTER 8

A Commotion in the House

The following morning, shortly after Sebastian had admitted the tutor, the door bell rang again, so loudly this time that the butler thought the master himself had arrived home unexpectedly. He rushed downstairs and threw open the door, and there stood a little ragged boy with a barrel organ on his shoulder.

"What do you want?" asked Sebastian irritably. "I'll teach you to ring the bell like that! Be off with you!"

"I want to see Clara," the urchin replied.

"You cheeky little brat. Don't you know to say *Fräulein* Clara? What could you possibly have to see Fräulein Clara about?" stormed Sebastian.

"She owes me fourpence," said the boy.

"You must be insane! What makes you think Fräulein Clara lives here, anyway?"

"Yesterday I showed her the way for twopence; and back again; that was fourpence."

"You are telling a pack of lies! Fräulein Clara never goes out—she can't walk. Be off with you now before I take my boot to you!"

But the boy was not to be turned away so easily. He stood firm and repeated determinedly, "But I have seen her in the street and can tell you what she looks like. She has short, curly hair and she wears a brown dress. She talks different from us."

"Ho!" thought Sebastian. "So this is more mischief the little fräulein has been up to!" He chuckled to himself as an idea occurred to him, then he said aloud, "Very well. Come with me, but wait outside the door until I call you, and when I let you into the room begin right away to play a tune on your barrel organ for the young lady. That will please her."

Sebastian knocked on the study door and went in. "There is a boy outside who says he has a message for Fräulein Clara," he announced.

This unexpected interruption to the lesson delighted Clara. "Let him come in at once!" she begged, turning to her tutor. "You see, he wants to speak to me particularly."

The boy entered, and at once started to play his organ according to Sebastian's instructions. Fräulein Rottenmeier was busy in the dining-room when the sound came to her ears. Was it in the street? Yet it seemed so much nearer! But who could be playing an organ in the study? And yet . . . She rushed into the study, and there, incredible as it seemed, there stood the ragged organ player. The tutor looked as though he were making an effort to speak, but failed. Clara and Heidi were listening happily.

"Stop! Stop at once!" commanded Fräulein Rottenmeier, but her voice was drowned by the music. She was walking towards the boy when suddenly on the floor between her feet she caught sight of a horrible, dark, crawling animal. It was a tortoise! At the sight of it, Fräulein Rottenmeier leaped into the air, shrieking at the top of her voice, "Sebastian! Sebastian!"

The organ player stopped abruptly. Sebastian stood behind the door, convulsed with laughter. At last he came in.

"Take them away! All of them! Boy, animal and all! At once, Sebastian!"

Sebastian dragged off the boy with the tortoise, at the same time putting something into his hand and whispering, "Fourpence for Fräulein Clara and fourpence for the music. You have done well!"

The door closed behind the little organ player, peace returned to the study and the lesson continued. This time Fräulein Rottenmeier remained in the room, grimly determined to prevent further incident.

Again a knock came to the study door and Sebastian appeared with the news that someone had brought a large basket to be delivered to Fräulein Clara. He carried in a covered basket and then disappeared.

"I think we will finish the lesson first," said Fräulein Rottenmeier, "and then we will see what is inside the basket."

Clara could not imagine what it could be and looked longingly at the basket. She broke off in the midst of her declinations to ask the tutor if she might have just one peep inside. The tutor frowned and was just about to refuse his permission when the lid of the basket lifted of its own accord and out jumped one, two, three, and then another two, and then several more kittens, and they all raced about

the room in every direction. They climbed up on to
Fräulein Rottenmeier's dress and scampered about
her feet. They climbed up on Clara's chair, and, in
fact, went into every corner of the room, scratching
and maiowing. Clara cried delightedly, "Oh, look at
them, Heidi! Aren't they sweet!"

Heidi raced about after them and the tutor, in a
dilemma, moved uncomfortably from one foot to
the other, at a complete loss to know what to do. At
first, Fräulein Rottenmeier was too horror-stricken
to utter a word, then she began to scream, "Tinette!
Sebastian! Sebastian! Tinette!" She was terrified to
move from her chair until Sebastian and Tinette
appeared at last and removed the kittens only to put
them in the basket with the others.

There had been no yawning during lessons that day.

In the evening, Fräulein Rottenmeier held an
inquiry into the affair. She summoned Sebastian
and Tinette and it soon became evident that Heidi,
on her excursion of the previous day, had been
responsible for all these alarming occurrences.
Fräulein Rottenmeier was pale with anger. She gave
a sign for Sebastian and Tinette to withdraw, then
she turned to Heidi who stood beside Clara's chair,
not very sure of what crime she had been guilty.

"Adelheid," Fräulein Rottenmeier began in a stern voice, "I know of only one punishment which will make you aware of your frightful misconduct for you are nothing but a little barbarian. We shall see if a spell down in the dark cellar with the rats and black beetles will tame you a little so that you will know not to do such things in future."

Heidi listened in silence and was rather surprised at the threatened punishment for she had never been in such a cellar. The room which the grandfather called the cellar at home was a very pleasant place where the fresh cheese and milk was kept.

But Clara started to cry, sobbing, "No! No! Fräulein Rottenmeier! You must wait till Papa comes home. He said in his letter that he would come back soon and when he does I will tell him everything and he shall decide what is to be done with Heidi."

Fräulein Rottenmeier was obliged to agree and she got up and left the room, grumbling, "Well, Clara, I too will have something to say to Herr Sesemann."

Although a few days passed quietly after this, Fräulein Rottenmeier failed to regain her peace of mind. She was constantly aware of the disappointment that Heidi had been and of the fact that since her arrival the whole household had been upset. But Clara was very happy indeed. She was never bored now, for during lessons something amusing was always happening. Instead of trying to learn the letters, Heidi would cry out, "Oh, it is shaped like a goat's horn!" or "It is like an eagle!" until the poor tutor would completely lose patience. Then, after lessons were over, in the late afternoon, Heidi would sit by Clara and tell her about the Alm and how much she wanted to go back. Indeed, she would talk about her old home until the longing to go back became so great that she would say, "I must go home again! To-morrow I must really go!" But Clara would persuade her to stay, saying, "Just wait until Papa comes home!" And Heidi would remember that each day she stayed meant that she could add another roll to her collection. Every night at supper she found a soft white roll on her plate and she would quietly slip it into her pocket. So she now had quite an amazing quantity of rolls to take back to the grandmother!

Every afternoon, while Clara rested, Heidi found herself alone and then she would sit by herself and think about the Alm. One day, the memory of the snowcapped peaks, the yellow flowers glittering in the sun, and the green valley made her feel so homesick that she could hardly control her longing to be home again. Dete, after all, had said that she could go home whenever she wanted. She hastily put the rolls into her red scarf, put on her little straw hat and started of for home. But she got no farther than the front door, for there stood Fräulein Rottenmeier, just returned from her walk. Her sharp eyes looked Heidi up and down. "What is the meaning of this? Didn't I forbid you to run about in the streets? And you are surely not going out dressed like a beggar child!"

"I wasn't going to run about, I just wanted to go home," explained Heidi, frightened.

"Wanted to go home, indeed! I wonder what Herr Sesemann would have to say to this? Running away from his beautiful house! What do you find wrong with it, I should like to know? Are you not treated better than you deserve? Have you ever in your life had such a splendid place to live in or had so many servants to wait upon you? Have you?"

"No," said Heidi.

"I should think not," continued the lady. "You

are an exceedingly ungrateful child who thinks of
nothing but getting into mischief."

This rebuke was too much for Heidi and she
began to pour out all the things that she had kept
hidden for so long. "I only want to go home
because Snowflake will be crying and the grandmother is waiting for me; and Goldfinch gets
beaten when Goat Peter doesn't get part of my
lunch. Here I can never watch the sun saying good
night to the mountains, and if the great bird were to
fly over Frankfurt he would croak even louder
about so many people huddling together, gossiping,
and not living in the mountains where it is so much
nicer."

"Mercy! The child has gone out of her mind!"
cried Fräulein Rottenmeier, rushing upstairs and
colliding with Sebastian. "Take the unfortunate
creature upstairs at once!" she called to him.

"What mischief have we been up to now, eh?"
said Sebastian good-humouredly. Heidi stood
trembling and frightened, and when Sebastian saw
the distress on her little face he said kindly, "Now,
now! Don't take it so much to heart! Cheer up and
everything will be all right! Come! We'd better do
as we were told and go upstairs."

Heidi looked such a picture of dejection as she slowly climbed the stairs that Sebastian felt really sorry for her. "Don't you give in!" he said encouragingly. "There's a brave little girl! Never a tear all the time she is with us, and others at her age cry twelve times a day. And the kittens are so happy! You should just see them jumping about in the loft! Afterwards we shall go up and look at them, together, shall we?—when madam is not here."

Heidi nodded, but not very cheerfully, and disappeared into her room.

At supper Fräulein Rottenmeier did not speak but kept casting very odd glances in Heidi's direction as though she expected the child to do something extraordinary at any moment. But Heidi sat silently at the table, neither eating nor drinking although the roll had, as usual, disappeared quickly into her pocket.

Next morning, when the tutor arrived, Fräulein Rottenmeier took him into the dining-room and told him her worries about Heidi and of her attempt to go home the previous day. "I really think the child has gone mad," she concluded. The tutor managed to quieten her fears, explaining that Adelheid was perhaps a little strange but with careful handling and education the balance would soon be restored. He was quite sure of this having now heard Fräulein Rottenmeier's revelation, and having so far failed to teach Heidi the alphabet. He felt that she was perhaps just a little eccentric, but it was nothing that perseverance would not cure.

Fräulein Rottenmeier felt quite relieved after this conversation and during the afternoon she began to recall Heidi's outlandish appearance when she had prepared to set out on her journey. She decided that the child had better have one or two things from Clara's wardrobe before Herr Sesemann arrived. Clara was completely in favour of the plan and the lady went into Heidi's room to inspect her wardrobe. Very soon she returned, wearing an expression of complete disgust. "Adelheid!" she said. "I have never seen anything like it! In a wardrobe of all places, what do I find? Heaps of little rolls! Who ever heard of keeping bread in a wardrobe? Tinette! Go and remove all that stale bread from Heidi's wardrobe—and you can take away the old straw hat, too! "

"No! No!" screamed Heidi. "Not the hat! And the rolls are for Grandmother!" And she began to

run after Tinette until Fräulein Rottenmeier
stopped her.

"Stay just where you are!" she said. "All that
rubbish must be thrown out."

Then Heidi threw herself into Clara's chair,
crying in despair. "Now Grandmother won't get
her rolls. She has taken them away!" and she
sobbed as though her heart would break.

Clara was very much alarmed at this outburst
and pleaded, "Heidi! Heidi! Don't cry! Listen to
me! I will give you as many rolls as you want when
you go home and they will be soft and fresh. Yours
were quite stale. Don't cry any more, Heidi!"

It was a long time before Heidi could stop
sobbing but Clara's promise had comforted her and
when she had assured herself that Clara would
indeed give her as many or more rolls than she had
collected, she quietened down.

At supper, Heidi's eyes were still swollen with
crying and when she looked at her roll she started to
sob again; but with a great effort she managed to
control herself for she knew that she had to be quiet
at table. Whenever Sebastian came near he smiled
at her encouragingly as if to say, "I will put everything right for you." He made signs at her all

evening, pointing to his head and hers, nodding and smiling.

When it came time for Heidi to go to bed, what did she find under the bed-cover but her old hat! She hugged it with delight, knocking it more out of shape than ever; then she wrapped it in a handkerchief and put it right at the back of the wardrobe. Sebastian had seen Tinette with the hat and had taken it from her quickly, saying, "It's all right. I shall dispose of this." This had been the reason for all the nods and smiles which Sebastian had given Heidi at supper.

CHAPTER 9

News from the Master

A few days later there was great excitement in the house because Herr Sesemann had returned. Sebastian and Tinette were kept busy carrying up parcels and suitcases from the carriage. They were packed with all sorts of exciting presents which Clara's father was in the habit of bringing back from his travels.

It was late afternoon when Herr Sesemann arrived and he came straight into the study where Clara and Heidi were sitting together. Father and daughter greeted each other affectionately for they loved each other very much, then Herr Sesemann held out his hand to Heidi and said kindly, "And this is our little Swiss girl? Come and shake hands with me? That's right! Now, you and Clara are

great friends, are you not? Or are you always quar-
relling with each other?"

"No, Clara is very good to me," answered Heidi.

"And Heidi," interjected Clara, "has never quar-
relled with me."

"That's good! I'm delighted to hear it," said Herr
Sesemann, rising from his chair. "Now, Clara, you
must allow me to go and have something to eat. I
have had nothing since breakfast. Later I shall see
you again and show you all the things I have
brought home."

In the dining-room he found Fräulein
Rottenmeier inspecting the table which had been
laid for dinner. Herr Sesemann sat down and
Fräulein Rottenmeier, looking the picture of gloom,
took her place opposite.

"What is the matter, Fräulein Rottenmeier?"
asked Herr Sesemann. "You look very dismal.
Have you had a stroke of bad luck? Clara seems to
be cheerful enough. What is wrong?"

With a very long face, the lady began, "Herr
Sesemann, we have been completely deceived—
and it concerns Clara."

"In what way?" Herr Sesemann asked calmly.

"You know we decided that Clara should have a

companion, and as I knew you were anxious to have
a nicely brought up girl, I thought of a little Swiss
girl of whom I had heard a great deal. You know
what I wanted—the sort of child of whom I often
read, who is so at ease living the natural life high in
the mountains, that she would be like a pure being
from another world!"

"And what do you think Clara would have in
common with such a person as you describe,
Fräulein?"

"I do not jest, Herr Sesemann. I have been terribly
cheated. Completely taken in! Really shockingly!"

"But what is so shocking? I see nothing shocking
in the child," remarked Herr Sesemann, still
completely unperturbed.

"Oh, if you only knew the type of people—and
the animals!— this creature has brought into your
house! The tutor can tell you all about it."

"Animals? What am I to understand from that,
Fräulein Rottenmeier"

"Herr Sesemann, it is beyond *my* understanding!
Her whole behaviour would be beyond comprehen-
sion were it not for one thing. She has spells of
mental   disturbance!"   concluded   Fräulein
Rottenmeier with conviction.

Up till now, Herr Sesemann had not thought the affair of any great importance; but mental disturbance! That could easily have a harmful effect on his little daughter.

He looked quickly at Fräulein Rottenmeier as though to assure himself that it was not she who was the victim of a troubled mind. Just then, the door opened and the tutor entered.

"Ah, here is our tutor! Perhaps he can clear this matter up for us," Herr Sesemann exclaimed. "Come, sit down and have a cup of coffee with us," he said, addressing the tutor. "No need for ceremony. Now tell me what is wrong with this child who has come to be a companion to my daughter. What's this about her bringing animals into the house, and about her mental faculties?"

The tutor began in his usual roundabout way, "Since you ask me for my opinion about this young girl, Herr Sesemann, I should like to direct your attention to the fact that, although there may be a lack of development, caused by more or less neglected education, or rather by somewhat delayed tuition, on the one hand, there is, on the other hand, I think we must admit, a certain

benefit to be gained from such a solitary life in the
mountains, and we must consider—"

"My dear friend," interrupted Herr Sesemann,
"you take too much trouble. Tell me, did her bringing animals to the house alarm you too, and what is
your opinion of her as a companion for my little
daughter?"

"I have no wish to say anything against the young
girl," the tutor began again. "If on the one hand
there is a certain inexperience of social custom,
owing to the somewhat uncivilised life she led up to
the time she came to Frankfurt, on the other hand
she has gifts not to be overlooked, and if carefully
led—"

"My dear sir, you must please excuse me now. I
must speak to my daughter." And with these words
Herr Sesemann quickly left the room.

In the study, he sat down beside his little girl and
turning to Heidi said, "Listen, little one, will you go
and fetch me—ah—fetch me—" Herr Sesemann
wanted the child out of the room but was having
difficulty in thinking up an excuse. "Fetch me a
glass of water?"

Heidi disappeared at once.

"And now, my dear Clara," said Herr Sesemann,

pulling his chair closer and taking his daughter's hand, "tell me quite frankly, what kind of animals did your little friend bring into the house? And what makes Fräulein Rottenmeier think that she is sometimes not quite right in her mind?"

Clara had no difficulty in explaining. She told her father the story of the tortoise and the kittens and explained all the remarks which Fräulein Rottenmeier had thought so odd, and which seemed to upset her so much.

Herr Sesemann laughed heartily. "Well, then, you don't want me to send the child home, Clara? You are not tired of her?" asked her father.

"No! No! Papa, please don't!" exclaimed Clara in alarm. "The time has passed so quickly since Heidi came. Something happens every day, and it used to be so dull. And she always has so much to tell me."

"Very well, then. Ah! Here is our little friend! Have you brought me nice fresh water?" Herr Sesemann asked as Heidi handed him the glass.

"Yes. It is fresh from the pump," answered Heidi.

"Did you go yourself to the pump, Heidi?" asked Clara.

"Yes, but I had to go a long way because at the first pump there were ever so many people and at the second there were just as many. Then I went into another street and got the water there. The gentleman with the white hair sends his kind regards to Herr Sesemann."

"Well, that was a long expedition," laughed Herr Sesemann. "And who is this gentleman?"

"As he was passing the pump he stopped and said, 'Since you have got a glass would you mind giving me a drink? To whom are you taking the glass of water?' And I said, 'To Herr Sesemann.' And he laughed and gave me the message for you and said he hoped Herr Sesemann would enjoy the water."

"And what did this gentleman look like who sends me so many good wishes?" asked Herr Sesemann with a smile.

"He wore a thick gold chain with a big red stone hanging from it; and the top of his stick was a horse's head."

"That is our old friend, the doctor," cried Clara and her father at the same instant. Herr Sesemann smiled to himself as he wondered what their friend would think of the new way in which the Sesemanns went about quenching their thirst.

That very evening, he told Fräulein Rottenmeier that Heidi would remain; that he found the child perfectly normal and that his daughter preferred her company to any other. "I am anxious, therefore," said Herr Sesemann emphatically, "that this child should always be treated in a friendly way and that her little peculiarities should not be treated as crimes. And, by the way, if you find difficulty in managing the child there is a prospect that you will be relieved of this duty. I am expecting my mother very soon for a long visit, and, as you know, she gets along with everybody, Fräulein Rottenmeier," he concluded pointedly.

"Yes, I know," Herr Sesemann," said Fräulein Rottenmeier rather sourly.

Herr Sesemann remained only a short time at home and after a fortnight he set off for Paris, comforting his little daughter with the prospect of the arrival of her grandmother in a day or two.

On the day after Herr Sesemann's departure, a letter came announcing Frau Sesemann's arrival on the following day. Clara was overjoyed and talked so much about her grandmother that Heidi, too, called her Grandmamma.

Later, when Heidi was going to her bedroom,

Fräulein Rottenmeier took her into her own room
and instructed her that she should never address
Frau Sesemann as Grandmamma but always as
'madam'. "Do you understand?" she asked.

Heidi really did not understand at all why she
should call the lady by this title but Fräulein
Rottenmeier's face wore such a severe expression
that Heidi did not dare ask for an explanation.

CHAPTER 10

Another Grandmother

The following evening great preparations were afoot in the Sesemann house. It was clear that the lady who was to arrive was held in great esteem by all and presently there was the sound of a carriage stopping at the front door. Sebastian and Tinette rushed downstairs and put footstools everywhere, that the lady might find one wherever she wanted to put her feet. Fräulein Rottenmeier followed, but slowly and with dignity. She knew that she would have to be there to welcome Frau Sesemann, but was not going to let her authority be undermined by the presence of another woman. Suddenly the carriage rolled up to the door, and the servants ran down the step to assist their important visitor. Heidi, who had been ordered to wait in her room until she was called, sat in a corner and repeated over and over again to herself the little speech which she had been instructed to address to Frau Sesemann.

Before very long Tinette came to call her. Putting her head round the door, she announced in her usual saucy manner "You're to go into the study."

Heidi made her way to the study, still turning the words over in her mind and still hardly able to believe that she should address any one in the peculiar way Fräulein Rottenmeier had told her. As she opened the door, the grandmother said in a kind voice, "Ah, here is the child! Come here and let me look at you!"

Heidi approached, and said very distinctly in her clear voice, "Good evening, Mrs madam!"

"Well," said the grandmother, laughing. "Is that how you address people on the Alm?"

"No. At home nobody has a name like that," said Heidi gravely.

"Neither do they here!" said the grandmother, still smiling, and patted Heidi's cheek. "When I am with children I am always Grandmamma. Can you remember that?"

"Yes, very well," Heidi assured her, "because that's what I used to say."

"I understand," said the grandmother, shaking her head a little. She looked more closely at Heidi and Heidi's steady, serious eyes looked back at her eagerly, for there was a warmth about the old woman which attracted the child. Heidi gazed entranced at the beautiful white hair which was adorned with a lacy frill, ending in two broad ribbons which floated gently about the grandmother's head as though blown by a soft breeze.

"And what is your name, child?"

"It is really Heidi, but if you call me Adelheid I shall try to remember—" Heidi stopped guiltily, remembering that sometimes she failed to answer when Fräulein Rottenmeier called her by this name. Just at that moment, Fräulein Rottenmeier entered.

"Frau Sesemann will agree that I had to choose a name which one could pronounce, and, of course, on account of the servants—"

"Very correct, I have no doubt, Rottenmeier," replied Frau Sesemann, "but if the child is called Heidi and is accustomed to that name, I shall call her by it; so that's settled."

Fräulein Rottenmeier found it very embarrassing

to be called by her surname but since the grand-mother would have her own way there was nothing she could do about it. She was a very alert old lady and had her wits about her, and she very soon knew exactly what was going on in the house.

The following afternoon, after sitting by Clara's bed until she fell asleep, Frau Sesemann went upstairs and knocked at Fräulein Rottenmeier's door. Fräulein Rottenmeier looked startled at this unexpected visit.

"Where is the Heidi child and what is she doing, I should like to know," said Frau Sesemann, coming straight to the point.

"She is in her room where she could find some-thing useful to do if she had the slightest inclina-tion," replied Fräulein Rottenmeier. "But if Frau Sesemann only knew the queer things she imagines and does—I can hardly bring myself to talk of them."

"And so would I, if I were in her place, I don't doubt. Tell the little one to come to my room. I have some nice books to give her."

"But that's just it!" replied Fräulein Rottenmeier, throwing up her hands in despair. "Of what use are books to her? She does not even know the alphabet

yet! It is quite impossible to teach her anything. The
tutor will tell you so himself. If he didn't have the
patience of a saint he would have given up trying to
teach her long ago."

"Well, that is strange. The child does not strike
me as being stupid," said Frau Sesemann shortly.
"Now go and fetch her. She can look at the pictures
for the time being."

Fräulein Rottenmeier was about to say more but
Frau Sesemann turned and went quickly into her
room. She was very surprised at Fräulein
Rottenmeier's remarks and was determined to find
out more about the whole matter. Perhaps the tutor
would help, although his conversation was so
roundabout and lengthy that she felt it might be
difficult to get to the root of the problem.

Heidi was greatly delighted with the beautiful
coloured pictures in the books which the grandmother had brought. Suddenly she cried aloud as
the grandmother turned a page, and when the old
lady looked at the child she saw that tears were
streaming down her cheeks. She looked at once at
the picture. It depicted a beautiful green pasture
with all sorts of animals grazing. In the midst, the
shepherd leant upon his stick and looked happily at

his flock. Everything was bathed in a golden light
for the sun was just setting on the far horizon.

The grandmother took Heidi's hand gently.
"Come, come! child! Don't cry! It has reminded
you of something, perhaps. But look, there is a
beautiful story about it and I am going to tell it to
you tonight. There are many beautiful stories in this
book which can be read over and over again. Come
now, we must have a chat, so dry your tears and
stand in front of me so that I can look at you. That's
right. Now we are happy again."

Heidi tried very hard to stop sobbing and when at
last she succeeded the grandmother said, "Now I
want you to tell me something, child. How are you
getting on with your lessons? Do you like them? Are
you doing well?"

"Oh, no!" answered Heidi with a sigh. "But I
knew it would be impossible."

"What is impossible, Heidi? What do you mean?"

"To learn to read. It is too difficult."

"Well I never! And who told you this?"

"Peter did, and he knows for he has tried and
tried but he can't learn. It is too difficult."

"What a boy Peter must be! But listen to me,
Heidi. We must never believe what the 'Peters' say

but try for ourselves. I am sure you have never paid
enough attention to the tutor or looked properly at
the letters."

"It is no use," said Heidi with a great sigh of
resignation.

"Now, Heidi. Listen to what I say! You have not
been able to learn to read because you believed
what Peter said. Now you must believe what I say
when I tell you that you can learn to read like many
other children who are like you and not like Peter,
and in a very short time. First you must know what
happens when you are able to read. Do you see the
shepherd on the beautiful green pasture? Well, as
soon as you can read you shall have the book for
your own and then you will know the whole story
just as if someone were to tell it to you—what the
shepherd did with his sheep and goats and the
wonderful things that happened to him. Wouldn't
you like to know all that, Heidi?"

Heidi had been listening with keen attention and
now exclaimed with sparkling eyes "Oh, if only I
could read already!"

"You will learn in no time—I can see that, Heidi.
But now we must go to Clara. Come, we will take
the books with us!"

The grandmother took Heidi's hand and they went together into the study.

From the day Heidi had tried to go home and Fräulein Rottenmeier had scolded her for being so wicked and ungrateful, a change had come over the child. She knew now that she could not go home whenever she liked, as Aunt Dete had told her, but that she had to stay in Frankfurt for a long time, maybe for ever. She also understood that Herr Sesemann would think her very ungrateful, and Clara and the grandmother, too, if she again showed signs of wanting to leave. So there was nobody to whom she could reveal how homesick she was, for she could not face giving the grandmother, who was so kind to her, cause to be angry, as Fräulein Rottenmeier had been.

But the strain of keeping all this to herself became almost more than she could bear. She lost her appetite and every day grew paler and paler. At night she would lie awake for a long time, for as soon as she was alone with everything quiet around her, she would see again in her thoughts the Alm and the sunshine and the flowers; and when at last she fell asleep she would see in her dreams the red summits of the crags and the crimson snowfield in

the evening sun. Awakening in the morning she
wanted to run out happily into the sun—but she
soon realised that she was in the big bed at
Frankfurt, far, far away from home. Then Heidi
would weep long and quietly, her head pressed into
the pillow so that no one could hear.

Heidi's unhappiness did not escape the grandmother. She waited a few days to see if there might
be a change. But as Heidi remained subdued and
when she noticed that often in the early morning
the child looked as though she had been crying, the
grandmother took her, one day, into her room and
said lovingly, "Now tell me, Heidi, what is the
matter? Are you worrying about something?"

But not for the world would Heidi show ingrati-
tude to the grandmother who had been so kind, so
she replied:

"Please, I cannot tell you."

"Could you tell Clara, then?"

"Oh, no! Nobody," said Heidi, looking so pitiful
that the grandmother was filled with compassion.

"Come here, little one, and I will tell you something. If one is in trouble and can't speak about it to
any one, then one tells it to God who is in Heaven
and prays to Him for help because he is able to take

away all our troubles. Do you know that? Do you pray every night to your Heavenly Father and thank Him for all he has done for you and ask Him to keep you from harm?"

"Oh, no! I never do that," answered Heidi.

"Have you never prayed, Heidi? Don't you know what it is?"

"Sometimes I used to pray with the first grandmother but it is a long time ago and I have forgotten it."

"You see, Heidi, because you have nobody to help you, you are unhappy. Think how wonderful it is when our hearts are heavy with sadness, to be able to go any moment to God and tell Him everything and ask Him for help when no one else can give it. He is always able to help and can give us what makes us happy again."

A gleam of joy came into Heidi's eyes, "May I tell Him everything?"

"Everything, Heidi. Everything."

Heidi drew away the hand which the grandmother held affectionately and asked hastily, "May I go?"

"Certainly, certainly!" answered the grandmother and Heidi ran off to her room. She sat down on her little stool, folded her hands and told God about everything that made her so unhappy and begged Him with all her heart to let her go home to the grandfather.

A little more than a week after this the tutor asked to see Frau Sesemann as he had something very remarkable to tell her. When he was shown into her room Frau Sesemann held out her hand, saying, "I am pleased to see you. Sit down, won't you? Now tell me why you wish to see me. I hope it is not a complaint."

"On the contrary, madam," the tutor began. "Something has occurred—something which I did not expect. In the light of all my previous experience it was an impossibility and yet it really has happened. It is like a miracle. Contrary to all I had expected—"

"Am I to understand that the child, Heidi, has learned to read after all?" Frau Sesemann guessed.

Speechless with surprise the tutor looked at her.

"It is indeed nothing short of a miracle. In spite of my painstaking explanations, she never seemed to be able to learn the alphabet, and now she has learnt it with such rapidity—overnight, so to say—and so correctly! It is most unusual with a beginner."

"Life is full of miracles," Frau Sesemann smiled. "Of course, there might be such a happy coincidence as a fresh zeal for learning and a new method of teaching. Now we must be glad the child has made such a good beginning and hope for her future progress."

After she had seen the tutor to the door, she went straight to the study to make sure of the good news. Sure enough, Heidi was seated beside Clara and was reading a story to her with great eagerness, evidently surprised herself to find the black letters turning into real people and exciting adventures.

That same evening, at the dinner table, Heidi found by her plate the big book with the lovely pictures and when she looked questioningly at the grandmother the old lady nodded her confirmation, "Yes, it is yours, now."

"Always? Even when I go home?" asked Heidi, flushed with happiness.

"Of course, for ever!" assured the grandmother. "To-morrow we shall start to read it."

"But you are not going home yet, Heidi," Clara put in. "Not for many years. I want you to stay with me, especially when grandmother goes away."

Before she went to bed, Heidi looked at her book, and from that day on, her greatest pleasure was to read over and over again the stories which belonged to the beautiful pictures.

When, in the evening, the grandmother said, "Now Heidi will read to us," the child was delighted and when she read aloud, the stories seemed to be still more beautiful and interesting. The picture she liked best was the one with the green pasture and the shepherd leaning happily on his crook. He was tending his father's fine flock. But the next picture showed how the shepherd had run away from home and had to look after a herd of swine. He had grown quite thin for all he had to eat was husks. In this picture, the sun did not shine so golden and the land was grey and misty. But then there was still another picture to this story. In it the old father was running with outstretched arms to meet his returning and repentant son, welcoming him as he approached timidly, tired and dirty and dressed in rags. This was Heidi's favourite story which she read again and again without ever tiring of hearing the grandmother's explanations of the meaning of the story. There were many other beautiful tales in the book, and with reading and studying the pictures the days passed quickly and the time came for the grandmother's departure.

CHAPTER 11

Heidi Learns a Great Deal

Every afternoon during her visit, the grand-mother sat beside Clara for a time while she was resting, and afterwards she would call Heidi into her room and would talk to her and keep her occupied in all sorts of ways. The grandmother had pretty little dolls and showed Heidi how to make little dresses and coats for them so that without knowing it Heidi had learnt to sew. Since Heidi could now read she was allowed to read aloud to the grandmother and this she enjoyed very much, growing more fond of the stories the more she read them. But still, Heidi never looked really happy and her sparkling eyes were never as bright as before.

One afternoon during the last week of the grand-mother's visit, when Heidi was paying her customary afternoon call, the grandmother asked, "Tell me, child, why is it you are not happy? Is there still the same grief in your heart?"

"Yes," Heidi nodded.

"Have you told God about it?"

"Yes."

"And do you say your prayers every day so that all will be well and you will be happy again?"

"Oh, no. I don't pray at all now."

"What is this, Heidi? Why don't you pray any more?"

"It is no use. God does not listen, and I can understand it; when there are so many people in Frankfurt all praying to Him, He cannot possibly listen to them all. He certainly has not heard me."

"What makes you so sure, Heidi?"

"I have prayed for the same thing every day for weeks and weeks and God has never done it."

"Oh, Heidi! That is not the way in which to think of Him. You see, God is our Heavenly Father and always knows what is best for us, even when we ourselves do not. If we ask for something which is not good for us, He does not grant it but instead gives us the thing that is best for us. If we go on praying earnestly and never run away or lose faith our prayers will be answered. You see, Heidi, what you asked for was not good for you just at the moment. God has certainly heard you. He can hear every one at the same time because He is God and not a human being like you or me. And because He knows what is good for you He says, 'Yes, Heidi shall have what she wants but only when it is good for her; because if I give her what she wants right away and then, by and by, she sees that it would have been better for her not to have had her own way, she will say, "If only God had not given me what I asked for! It is not so good as I thought."' Since God watched over you, you should have trusted in Him, come with everything to Him and prayed every day; but you ran away, stopped praying and forgot all about Him!

"But you see, when someone behaves like you so that God never hears his voice among those who pray, He lets him go his own way. And when he gets into trouble and then complains, 'There is no one to help me!' God says, 'Why did you run away from Me? I cannot help you when you run away.' Do you want that, Heidi? Or would you rather go and ask Him to forgive you for running away, and pray to Him every day and trust that He will make everything right for you and that you will be happy again?"

Every word the grandmother said had touched the child's heart and she said repentantly, "At once I will ask God to forgive me and I will never forget Him again. I will go and pray now."

"That is a good child. He will help you at the right moment, never fear!" And Heidi ran to her room and prayed to God to forgive her and asked Him not to forget her.

It was a sad time for Clara and Heidi when the day of the grandmother's departure arrived, but the old lady insisted on making it quite a party so that they would not think too much about her going. After the grandmother had driven off in her carriage the house seemed very empty and silent and Clara and Heidi felt quite lost.

The next day, when the children sat together in the afternoon, Heidi suggested to Clara that she should read aloud to her every afternoon. Clara was very pleased with this idea and Heidi began with great enthusiasm. But the first story turned out to be about a dying grandmother and Heidi, who took all the stories very seriously and believed every word was true, at once thought that it was the grandmother on the Alm who was dead and burst into tears. Clara tried to explain that the story was about a quite different grandmother, but the idea that such a thing could happen had entered Heidi's mind and she realised with a great shock that the grandmother and the grandfather also might die while she was so far away and if she did not go home for a very long time everything on the Alm might be silent and dead and she would be all alone and would never see her dear ones again. And these sad thoughts made her sob the louder.

In the midst of Clara's explanation Fräulein Rottenmeier had entered the room and as Heidi still continued to sob she burst out impatiently, "Adelheid! That will do! I warn you, if you continue to give way to these outbursts whenever you read I will take the book away from you for good."

Heidi turned pale at such a thought. The book was her most treasured possession. Hurriedly she dried her tears. The stratagem had worked all right. No matter what the story, Heidi never cried again. But sometimes it was so difficult to keep back the tears that Clara would say, "Heidi, what terrible faces you are making!" But grimaces made no noise and did not attract Fräulein Rottenmeier's attention.

Heidi began to lose her appetite again and grew so pale and thin that Sebastian was extremely perturbed when she refused to take any of the delicious food which he served. Often he would whisper encouragingly as he held out a dish, "Take a little of this, Fräulein Heidi! It is so good! No, not like that! A heaped spoonful, and another one!" and other pieces of fatherly advice. But it was no use. Heidi hardly ate anything and as she lay in bed at night she would begin to think about home and what might be happening there, and she would turn her face into her pillow so that no one would hear, and cry as though her heart would break.

The days went by and Heidi could hardly tell whether it were winter or summer, for all she ever saw of the outside world was the same grey walls and roofs. She was only allowed out when Clara was well enough to go for a short drive (which never took them farther than the neighbouring streets) and never had a glimpse of grass or flowers, let alone fir trees and mountains. Heidi's longing for the beautiful, remembered things grew every day so that she could not speak or think of them without her eyes filling with tears.

Autumn and winter passed and the spring sun
shone on the white walls of the house opposite, and
Heidi knew it would soon be the time when Peter
climbed up to the Alm with his goats, the flowers
glittered in the sunshine and in the evening the
mountains turned to crimson in the setting sun.
Heidi would sit in her lonely little room and press
her palms into her eyes so that she would not be
able to see the sunshine striking the wall, and so she
sat, silently struggling against her homesickness
until she heard Clara's voice calling her.

CHAPTER 12

The House is Haunted

For some time, very strange things had been happening in the house. Every morning when the servants came down they found the front door wide open. During the first few days when this had happened all the rooms in the house were carefully searched for signs of burglary, but nothing was missing. At night every care was taken. The door was carefully locked and bolted, and to make it even more secure the wooden bar was put across. But all these precautions were of no avail; in the morning, the servants would again find the door wide open. Fräulein Rottenmeier would never go alone to some parts of the house, and would invent some excuse for one of the servants to accompany her. She was especially nervous if she had to visit the upper guest rooms, or go down to the strange, vast council chambers, where every footfall sounded and the ancient senators in their austere robes looked down sternly at her.

The cook meanwhile, would stand by her stove, shaking her head and muttering to herself, "To think that I should live to see such strange goings-on." At last John and Sebastian plucked up courage and promised to sit up all night in the room off the hall and watch to see what took place. Fräulein Rottenmeier, thinking they should be armed against any intruders, got out two of Herr Sesemann's pistols, and brought up a bottle of wine from the cellar with which the watchers might fortify their courage.

On the appointed night, the two installed themselves in the downstairs room and at once felt in need of a little stimulant. At first the wine made them very talkative, and by and by very sleepy, so they both leaned back in their arm-chairs and fell fast asleep. Sebastian awoke as the old church clock struck midnight. He called to his companion but John remained fast asleep. Sebastian did not go to sleep again but sat uneasily in the quietness of the night, only now and then giving John a quiet poke to see if he were awake. The clock struck the hour and John awoke with a start. He jumped to his feet and with a great show of courage said, "Now, Sebastian, we had better go outside and see what is going on. You aren't feeling scared, are you? Come on! I'll go first."

John opened the door wide and stepped into the hall. A sudden draught put out the light which he carried and he turned quickly, pushing against Sebastian, and stumbled back into the room, slamming the door and turning the key in the lock with feverish haste. Then he relit the candle. Sebastian did not know what to make of this odd behaviour and turned a puzzled look on John. In the light of the candle he saw that John was as white as a sheet and trembled all over. "What is it?" Sebastian asked hurriedly. "What did you see?"

"The door wide open," gasped John, "and on the stairs, a white figure—then, poof! and it was gone."

Sebastian shuddered with horror and felt as though his knees were going to give way. For the rest of the night the two sat close together and did not move again until the morning light came streaming through the window and the sound of passers-by came from the street. Then they went out and closed the front door and made their way upstairs to tell their story to Fräulein Rottenmeier. Straight away, she wrote a long letter to Herr Sesemann, telling him all about the open door and the ghostly figure, and insisting upon his immediate return as every one in the house now went in fear of his life and there was no knowing what the dreadful consequences of these incidents might be. But Herr Sesemann replied that it was impossible for him to return home just then, and altogether treated the affair very lightly. He suggested that should the ghost not have already disappeared, the grandmother should be summoned by letter to come and dispense with the nuisance.

Fräulein Rottenmeier was not at all satisfied. She wrote immediately to Frau Sesemann, but received a similarly indifferent reaction, and the tone of the letter, was to her mind, quite uncivil. Frau Sesemann implied that she did not care to undertake the journey from Holstein to Frankfurt, simply because Rottenmeier imagined she saw ghosts. She had never known a ghost in the house, and if there was now one in residence, it must be alive, in which case Rottenmeier should be able to deal with it.

Fräulein Rottenmeier was beginning to feel that

she had had quite enough of this particular worry.
She had never told the children of the apparition for
fear of upsetting them, but now she had an idea. In
a hushed voice and with much colourful detail, she
told them of the nightly visitations. The story so
frightened Clara that she began to scream for her
father to come home. She was in such a state of
fright that she would not be left alone for a minute.
She insisted that everyone should sleep in the same
room, and leave the light burning all the time; and
Tinette should be next door, and Sebastian and
John upstairs in the hall in order to frighten the
ghost as soon as it appeared. Fräulein Rottenmeier
wrote another letter to Herr Sesemann saying she
would not answer for the serious consequences the
mysterious occurrences might have on his daugh-
ters's delicate constitution. This had the desired
effect.

Two days later Herr Sesemann came home. He
stood and rang the front door-bell in such a way
that everyone rushed down and stood trembling as
if they thought the ghost was up to his tricks in
broad daylight.

Sebastian peered through a window, and at once
there was another, very human and impatient ring

on the bell. Clara was over-joyed to see him, and
when he saw in what good spirits she was, a look of
great relief spread over his features. Indeed, she was
so pleased to see him that she was almost grateful to
the ghost, for being responsible for his homecoming.

"And how is the ghost behaving?" he asked
Fräulein Rottenmeier with a twinkle in his eye.

"It is no joke," she replied tartly. "I am sure by
to-morrow Herr Sesemann will no longer consider
it a laughing matter."

"Well, we shall see," replied Herr Sesemann,
"but I must request you not to suspect my
honourable forefathers. Now send Sebastian to
me."

Herr Sesemann knew that Sebastian and
Fräulein Rottenmeier were not always on the best
of terms and he had his own ideas as to the cause of
the disturbances.

"Now, Sebastian," he said, "tell me frankly.
Have you been playing ghosts to tease Fräulein
Rottenmeier?"

"On my honour, sir, no," replied Sebastian with
unmistakable sincerity; "Please don't think that! I
have been feeling very uncomfortable myself about
this thing."

"Well, if that is so, I will have to show you and the brave John how ghosts look in the daylight. You should be ashamed of yourself, Sebastian, a big strong fellow like you running away from a ghost! But now go at once to my old friend Dr. Classen. Give him my kind regards and ask him to come here to-night at nine o'clock. Tell him I have come specially from Paris to consult him and will he make arrangements to spend the night here. Do you understand?" Sebastian indicated that he understood perfectly, and Herr Sesemann went to reassure Clara, telling her that the ghost would soon be found out and done away with.

Promptly at nine o'clock the doctor arrived after both Fräulein Rottenmeier and the children had gone to bed. He was a grey-haired man with bright, kindly eyes. At first he looked a little worried but presently he burst out laughing. "Well, well! For a patient with whom I am to sit up all night you don't look too bad."

"Not so hasty, my friend. Wait until I tell you this. There's a ghost in the house! This place is haunted."

The doctor laughed uproariously.

"That's a fine way of showing your sympathy I

must say," Herr Sesemann continued. "It's a pity my friend Rottenmeier can't enjoy it. She is convinced that some ancient member of the family is prowling about the house."

"And how did she make his acquaintance?" asked the doctor, still chuckling. Herr Sesemann told him how the front door was found open every morning, as everyone in the house was willing to swear, and he had prepared two loaded revolvers in readiness for any untoward event. It could be that an elaborate practical joke was being played by a friend of one of the servants—in which case a pistol shot would frighten him sufficiently, or it was a thief, thinking to create safe access for himself at a future time, by pretending to be a ghost with whom everyone would become familiar and used to seeing in the house.

When the doctor had heard the whole story the two gentlemen went downstairs to the room where Sebastian and John had kept watch. There, a bottle of wine was put at their disposal, and the two revolvers together with two large lamps. They settled themselves comfortably in arm-chairs and smoked and chatted together with such enjoyment that in what seemed no time at all they heard the clock strike twelve.

"The ghost seems to have got wind of us and does not choose to come to-night," said the doctor.

"Hold on! It usually comes before one o'clock," replied his friend.

They resumed their conversation and until one o'clock struck there was not a sound to be heard. Then suddenly the doctor lifted a-finger.

"Hush, Sesemann. Don't you hear something?"

They both listened and heard distinctly the bar on the door being softly pushed aside, the key turning in the lock and the door opening. Herr Sesemann seized one of the pistols which lay ready on the table.

"You are not afraid are you?" whispered the doctor.

"As well to be careful," Herr Sesemann replied, picking up the lamp. The doctor took the other pistol and together they stepped out into the hall.

Moonlight streamed through the open door and fell on a white figure which stood motionless on the threshold.

"Who is there?" the doctor demanded loudly, his voice echoing through the hall. As both gentlemen advanced towards the figure it turned and gave a little cry. In her little white nightgown and with her bare feet, Heidi stood there trembling and blinking at the light and the weapons pointed in her direction.

The gentlemen exchanged surprised glances.

"Well if it isn't the little water-carrier!" said the doctor.

"Child, what does this mean?" asked Herr Sesemann. "Why have you come downstairs?"

Pale and trembling with fright, Heidi stood before him. "I don't know," she whispered.

Then the doctor intervened. "Sesemann, this is something I shall have to deal with. Go and sit by the fire while I take the child up to bed."

The doctor put down his revolver and taking the child in his arms he carried her upstairs, reassuring her gently all the while, and laying her on her bed he covered her carefully with the quilt. Then he sat on the edge of the bed, and taking her hand, he said kindly, "Everything is all right now. Tell me where you wanted to go."

"I didn't want to go at all," said Heidi. "I didn't know I was going downstairs but suddenly I was there."

"Were you dreaming about something which you could see and hear everything as if you were there?"

"Yes, I dream every night and it is always the same. I think I am with Grandfather and outside I hear the fir trees rustling and I think how beautifully the stars will be shining and I run quickly and open the door of the cottage. But when I awake I am still in Frankfurt." Heidi struggled to swallow the lump which rose in her throat.

"And have you a pain anywhere? In your head or in your back?"

"No. Only a feeling as if there were a big stone here."

"As though you had eaten something and it would not go down?"

"No, not like that. But so heavy that it makes me want to cry and cry."

"I see, and then you have a good cry?"

"Oh, no, I mustn't. Fräulein Rottenmeier doesn't allow it."

"Then you just swallow hard, is that it? But you like being in Frankfurt, don't you?"

"Yes," said Heidi in a flat voice which made it sound more like 'no'.

"And where did you live when you were with your grandfather?"

"Always on the Alm."

"And wasn't that rather dull?"

"Oh, no, it was beautiful. It was so beautiful—" Heidi could not go on. Remembrance of the past, the recent excitement and the long-suppressed weeping overwhelmed the child. Tears gushed from her eyes and her little body was shaken with sobs. The doctor rose. Gently he laid Heidi's head on the pillow. "Cry a little. It will do no harm, and then sleep. To-morrow everything will be all right."

The doctor went downstairs and joined his friend. He lowered himself into the opposite arm-chair and looked across at him gravely. "Sesemann, your little protégé is a sleep-walker. Every night, without knowing it, she has been opening the front door and alarming your staff. The child is pining away with homesickness. Didn't you see how pathetically thin she is? Now there is only one remedy for her overstretched nerves, and that is to send her back home at once. My advice is that the child should travel home to-morrow."

Herr Sesemann got up in a great state of agitation and strode up and down the room. "Ill, Homesick! Wasting away! In my house! And nobody seems to have noticed it! And you, doctor, suggest that I should send her back home in that pathetic state.

No, doctor, I cannot do it. You take the child in hand and restore her to health; then I shall send her home if she wants to go."

"Sesemann," said the doctor, "consider! This is not an illness that can be cured with pills and powders. The child does not have a strong constitution but if she gets back home to the mountain air she will very quickly recover; if not—wouldn't you rather send the child back ill than not at all?"

Such blunt words alarmed Herr Sesemann and he agreed at once. "Well, if you think that is the only way then we must act at once." They discussed the matter further and after a while the doctor took his leave. When the master of the house opened the door the bright morning light shone in.

CHAPTER 13

Back to the Alm

In great agitation, Herr Sesemann went upstairs to Fräulein Rottenmeier's room. His loud rap on the door awakened the lady and she was startled to hear him say, "Come down to the dining-room quickly, please! We must make preparations for a journey."

Fräulein Rottenmeier had never before been obliged to get up so early. It was only half-past four in the morning. What could possibly have happened? She was so flustered that she could hardly manage to dress. Herr Sesemann proceeded to rouse the whole staff and his urgent cries convinced them that the ghost had attacked the master and he needed their help. But, to their surprise, they found him walking up and down in the dining-room and not looking at all terrified. John was ordered to get the horses and carriage ready; Tinette had to wake Heidi and help her to dress and Sebastian was sent off to the house where Dete was in service, to bring her along.

At last Fräulein Rottenmeier was ready and came downstairs although she had put her cap on back to front in her hurry of preparation. Herr Sesemann instructed her to pack a trunk with the Swiss child's belongings and to add one or two things of Clara's so that the child would have some decent clothes to go home with. All this had to be done at once, Herr Sesemann insisted.

Poor Fräulein Rottenmeier stared in bewilderment at Herr Sesemann. She had expected to hear a hair-raising account of an encounter with a ghost in which she would have revelled in broad daylight and instead she was being given these practical instructions. Unable to believe her ears, she waited silently for Herr Sesemann to say something further; but he had no time for lengthy explanations and bustled off to Clara's room, leaving her standing there. He found Clara lying awake, wondering what could be the cause of such an upheaval in the house. Sitting beside her bed, her father told her all

that had happened; about the doctor's verdict and
how he thought that as Heidi was in a very over-
wrought state her sleep walking might take her
somewhere dangerous. So they had decided to send
Heidi home again at once.

Clara was distressed and made all sorts of sugges-
tions for keeping Heidi with her, but her father
remained firm, promising that if she were a good
girl and did not make a fuss he would take her to
Switzerland the following year. Eventually Clara
gave in to him, on condition that Heidi's box would
be packed in her room so that it would be possible
for Clara to add things to it if she wanted.

In the meantime, Dete had arrived and was waiting downstairs wondering what on earth had
happened that she should be summoned at such an
early hour. Herr Sesemann told her about Heidi
and that she was to go home that very day, accompanied by Dete herself.

Dete was very disappointed for this was the last
thing she had expected to hear. She recalled the
Uncle saying that he never wished to see her again,
and it occurred to her that it would not be a safe
undertaking to once again take the child to him,
having once already delivered her and taken her

away. Quickly she made as many excuses as she could muster, speaking low and fluently, so that Herr Sesemann, sensing her reluctance, told her to go away.

Herr Sesemann told Sebastian that he would have to accompany the child on her journey, the first day as far as Basle and the next day to her destination. He would be furnished with an explanatory letter to the grandfather, after presenting which he could return at once.

"But the main thing is this, Sebastian," concluded Herr Sesemann, "and I want you to see it is carried out. On this card I have written the name of the hotel in Basle. Show it to the manager and you will be given accommodation for the child and yourself. Go into the child's room and see that the windows are securely fastened, and when he has gone to bed, lock the door from the outside, for the child is a sleep-walker."

"Ah, so that was the ghost! I understand!" exclaimed Sebastian in great surprise.

"Yes, you foolish fellow. What cowards you all were," said Herr Sesemann and went off to his room to write a letter to the Alm-Uncle. Sebastian stayed where he was, feeling sheepish, and wishing

.that he had not let John drag him back into the
room, instead of going after the small white figure.
"I should certainly follow it if I saw it now," he said
to himself. But of course everything was clearly illu-
minated by daylight.

All this time, Heidi was completely ignorant of
what was afoot and was standing dressed in her
Sunday best without the faintest notion why.
Tinette had helped her to dress without uttering a
word, for she considered her a common child and
not fit to be spoken to.

The letter written, Herr Sesemann returned to
the dining-room where breakfast was ready, and
demanded, "Where is the child?"

Heidi was fetched and as she said good morning,
Herr Sesemann looked into her sad little face. "Now
what do you say to this, little one?" he asked kindly.

Heidi looked at him in surprise.

"Don't you know about it yet?" Herr Sesemann
laughed. "You are going home to-day."

"Home?" repeated Heidi faintly, turning pale.
For a moment she could hardly breathe, she was so
overcome by the news.

"Perhaps you don't want to go," suggested Herr
Sesemann.

"Oh, yes, I do want to go home," she replied, her face aglow with pleasure.

"Very well, then, you must take a good breakfast and then off you go in the carriage."

But hard as she tried, Heidi could scarcely swallow a mouthful for excitement. It all seemed like a dream and she thought that at any moment she might wake and find herself at the front door, shivering in her nightgown.

"Tell Sebastian to take plenty of provisions, for naturally the child can't eat just at present," Herr Sesemann told Fräulein Rottenmeier, who just at that moment entered the room. And turning to Heidi, he said kindly, "Go and join Clara until the carriage arrives."

Heidi rose eagerly and ran upstairs to Clara's room. In the middle of the floor was a big trunk which Clara had packed with dresses, pinafores, handkerchiefs and all sorts of clothes. "Look what I have packed for you," said Clara "Aren't you pleased, Heidi? And look, Heidi!" Triumphantly she held up a basket. Heidi peeped in and jumped for joy, for inside were twelve beautiful white rolls for the grandmother.

The children were so happily absorbed in their

preparations that they had forgotten completely that the time for parting had come, and when the carriage was ready there was no time left for sadness.

Remembering her favourite book, Heidi ran back quickly to her own room and took it from under the pillow, the place where she always kept it, and racing back she put it into the basket with the rolls. Then she went and had a last look in the wardrobe and, sure enough, there was her old red shawl, which Fräulein Rottenmeier had not thought worth including with the rest of her luggage. Heidi wrapped it up and carefully hid it amongst the other luggage so that it would not be seen.

The children had to say good-bye quickly for Herr Sesemann was waiting to see Heidi to the carriage. Fräulein Rottenmeier was waiting at the top of the stairs and somehow a peep of red amongst Heidi's luggage caught her eye. She at once pulled out the red shawl and threw it aside.

"No, Adelheid," she scolded, "you cannot possibly take that old thing with you. Good-bye, then!"

Heidi did not dare lift up the little bundle but looked imploringly at the master of the house with an expression which suggested that her greatest treasure had been taken from her.

"No, no," objected Herr Sesemann very firmly. "The child can take home whatever she pleases, whether it be kittens or tortoises and we won't be upset about it either, Fräulein Rottenmeier."

Heidi quickly lifted up her bundle and her eyes beamed with gratitude. Herr Sesemann shook hands with her, wished her a happy journey and said that he and Clara would always remember her. Heidi thanked him for all his kindness and said finally, "And please say good-bye to the doctor for me and thank him very, very much." She had not forgotten his words of the night before when he had said, "And to-morrow everything will be all right." And now these words had really come true and Heidi was convinced that it was all of his doing.

She was lifted into the carriage, and trunk, basket and provisions followed. Finally Sebastian climbed up beside her. Once more Herr Sesemann wished her a good journey and the carriage rolled away.

Very soon Heidi was sitting beside Sebastian in the train, her basket on her lap. She would not let go of it for a second, for inside were the rolls for the Grandmother. For many hours she sat silent. Only

now did she fully realise that she was on her way
home to the grandfather, the grandmother and
Goat Peter; and the familiar scene rose before her
eyes. She thought of how beautiful everything
would look at home, but then a sudden thought
came to her and suddenly she turned anxiously to
Sebastian. "Sebastian, are you sure the grandmother on the Alm is not dead?"

"No, no," he replied comfortingly, "I am sure she
will still be alive."

Once more Heidi became preoccupied with her
own thoughts, occasionally peeping into the basket.
After some time she asked again, "Sebastian, if I
only knew for certain that grandmother is still
alive!"

"Yes, yes," said Sebastian, half asleep. "She will
be alive. Why should she be dead?"

After a while Heidi fell asleep, too, and slept so
soundly that she did not wake up until Sebastian
shook her by the arm and said, "Wake up! Wake
up! We are in Basle. This is where we get out!"

The next morning they had to start again on a
long train journey, and as they reached their desti-
nations Heidi was too excited to talk and again sat
with her basket held tightly. When she least

expected it, a voice shouted, "Mayenfeld!" Up she jumped from her seat and Sebastian followed. As they stood on the platform beside Heidi's luggage, Sebastian looked regretfully after the disappearing train, for he much preferred that comfortable mode of transport to the tiring and dangerous climb up into the mountains in this, as he considered it, barbarous country. Cautiously he looked round to see of whom he might inquire the safest road to Dörfli. He spotted a broad-shouldered man loading a cart with big heavy sacks which had just arrived by train. Sebastian addressed his inquiry to him.

"All the roads here are safe," answered the man.

So Sebastian asked which was the best way one could take without being in danger of falling over a precipice, and also how to get a trunk up to Dörfli. The man regarded the trunk and then declared that if it was not too heavy, he would take it on his cart, as he was on his way there. After further conversation, the man agreed to take both the child and the trunk as far as Dörfli and from there somebody would take her up to the Alm.

"I can go by myself. I know the way from Dörfli to the Alm," said Heidi, who had been listening attentively to the conversation.

Sebastian was greatly relieved not to have to do any climbing. He took Heidi aside and gave her a heavy little leather bag and the letter to the grandfather, explaining; "This little bag is a present from Herr Sesemann. It must go to the bottom of the basket, under the rolls, and the little fräulein must be very careful with it for Herr Sesemann would be very angry if she were to lose it."

"I won't lose it," said Heidi confidently and at once put both the bag and the letter at the bottom of her basket.

The trunk was hoisted on to the cart and then Sebastian helped Heidi with her basket on to the driver's seat. He shook hands with her and reminded her once more about the contents of the basket. (Sebastian was rather worried as he knew he was supposed to see the child right to her destination.) The driver swung himself up beside Heidi and the cart moved off. Sebastian, glad to have rid himself of a wearisome duty, sat down in the station to wait for the return train.

The man with the cart was the miller from Dörfli who was taking home his sacks of flour. He had never seen Heidi before but felt sure this must be the much-discussed child whose parents he had known. He began to wonder what had happened that she should be returning here. "Aren't you the little girl who lived with the uncle on the Alm?" he shouted to Heidi above the noise of the cart.

"Yes," replied Heidi.

"You are soon back, aren't you? Didn't they treat you well there?"

"No, it wasn't that. Nobody could have been treated better than I was in Frankfurt."

"What brings you back then?"

"Because Herr Sesemann allowed me."

"But wouldn't you rather have stayed?"

"Oh, I'd rather be with the grandfather on the Alm than anywhere else in the world!"

"Maybe you'll think differently once you're there," muttered the baker, and then said to himself, "It's very odd, she must surely know what it's like up there." Then he started to whistle and said no more.

Heidi looked round and trembled with excitement as she began to recognise the trees on the road and above, the great towering peaks which seemed to welcome her back like old friends. Heidi nodded to them in turn, and at every bend of the road grew more and more happy until she felt she would burst with joy. More than anything she wanted to leap from the plodding cart and run as fast as she could until she reached the Alm. But instead, she sat still and patient, despite her inward excitement. As they drove into Dörfli the clock was striking five. A group of women and children clustered round the cart and wanted to know where they had come from and where they were going. As the baker lifted Heidi down she said quickly, "Thank you. Grandfather will fetch the trunk later," and tried to run off. She was at once stopped by questions from all sides but she pushed her way through the crowd with such a worried expression that the people were compelled to stand aside and let her through. It was certain, in their minds, that she would not go back to the grandfather if she had anywhere else to go, but the baker quickly enlightened them, declaring that although she had had the chance to live in a house where she had everything, it was her own wish to return to the grandfather. "There you are," they said to each other, "you can see she's frightened, and no wonder." They whispered about the Alm-Uncle and how he had deteriorated during the year, never saying one word, and looking like thunder at those he met. This news amazed everybody and it was soon spread around Dörfli that Heidi had given up a luxurious home to return to the hut on the Alm.

As fast as she could, Heidi climbed up from Dörfli. As she reached the top the path got steeper and the basket seemed to get heavier and heavier, so that she was obliged to pause now and then to get her breath. There was only one thought in her mind. Would she find the grandmother still in her usual corner by the spinning wheel? Suddenly she caught sight of the cottage and her heart began to pound. She ran as fast as she could until she reached the door ant trembled so much with excitement that she could hardly open it. But then she was inside and standing in the middle of the little room with no breath left to say a word.

"Dear Lord!" a voice cried from the corner, "that sounded like Heidi. If only I could have her with me again. Who is there?"

"But it *is* Heidi, Grandmother! I am back!" called Heidi and rushed towards the old woman. She put her arms round her and hugged her, unable to speak for joy. At first the grandmother was too overwhelmed to utter a word; then she caressed Heidi's curly head and said, "It is her hair, and her voice. Thank God that He has granted this to me!" Tears of joy spilled from her blind eyes. "Is it really you, Heidi? Have you come back to me?"

"Yes, Grandmother, it is true," assured Heidi. "Don't cry. I am really back and will come to you every day and never go away again. And you won't have to eat hard bread for a while. Look, Grandmother, look!"

Heidi unpacked her basket and piled the twelve rolls in the grandmother's lap.

"Ah, child, what a blessing you bring with you," she said, feeling the rolls, of which there seemed to

be a countless number, but the greatest blessing is
you yourself," and again she touched Heidi's hair
and her hot cheek. "Speak to me, child," she
murmured, "so that I can hear your voice again."

Heidi was in the midst of telling the grandmother
how she had feared she might never see her again
when the door opened and Peter's mother walked
in. For a moment she stood perplexed, then she
cried, "Can it possibly be you, Heidi?"

Brigitta's quick glance soon took in Heidi's
appearance, and with little gasps of admiration she
exclaimed to the grandmother, "Mother, if you
could only see what a pretty frock she is wearing
and how grand she looks! I hardly recognise her.
And this hat with the feather, is it yours, too, Heidi?
Put it on and let me see how you look in it."

"No, I don't care about it," replied Heidi. "If you
like it, please have it. I still have my old one." Heidi
opened the little red bundle and took out her own
hat which looked more crushed than ever after the
long journey. But that did not trouble Heidi. She
still remembered all the grandfather had had to say
about hats with feathers, on Dete's last visit. This
was why she had looked after her old hat so
lovingly, for she had always the thought of going

home again in the back of her mind. And taking off her pretty frock, she wrapped the red shawl round her shoulders. "But now," she said, taking the grandmother's hand, "I must go home to Grandfather. To-morrow I shall come back. Good night, Grandmother!"

"Yes, come again, Heidi, come again to-morrow," begged the grandmother and pressed the child's hands.

"But why have you taken off your pretty dress?" Brigitta wanted to know.

"Because I would rather go to Grandfather like this in case he shouldn't recognise me. You hardly new me at first."

Brigitta thought she was silly, and told her not to give it away. Perhaps Heidi should sell it to the schoolmaster's daughter in Dörfli. But Heidi did not change her mind, and later hid the hat behind the grandmother's chair. Brigitta accompanied her to the door and there said to her, "You could have kept the dress, he would have recognised you; but approach him carefully, for Peter says that Alm-Uncle never talks to anyone these days and is very moody."

Heidi said good night and went off up to the Alm.

The big snow-field at the Scesaplana sparkled in the evening sun. A red shimmer fell on the grass at Heidi's feet and she turned round. She had not remembered, even in her dreams, how beautiful this picture was. The two peaks of the Falkins rose like twin flames, the snowfield was aglow and above it floated rose-tinted clouds. Far below stretched the valley, and above and around everything glittered and sparkled. Tears crept down Heidi's cheeks at the sight of all this splendour. Earnestly she pressed her hands together and thanked God for bringing her home again. She stood still, her heart full of thankfulness, until the light began to fade, and then all at once she ran up the mountain as fast as she could. Presently the tops of the fir trees waving in the wind and then the hut came into view, and there was the grandfather sitting on his bench and smoking his pipe. Heidi ran faster and before the Alm-Uncle was aware of anything Heidi had thrown her basket to the ground and put her two arms round his neck, unable to say more than, "Grandfather! Grandfather! Grandfather!"

The old man could say nothing. For the first time for many years his eyes were wet with tears and he brushed them roughly away with the back of his hand. Then he lifted Heidi on to his knee and looked at her. "So you have come home again to me, Heidi," he began. "You don't look very much of a lady. Did they send you away?"

"Oh, no, Grandfather. You mustn't think that. They were all very good to me, Clara and Grandmamma and Herr Sesemann. It was just that I couldn't bear being away from you any longer. Sometimes I felt I would choke, but I never said anything because it would have been ungrateful. Then suddenly one morning Herr Sesemann called for me very early—I think maybe it was the doctor who told him—but perhaps it is all in the letter—" and Heidi jumped down and fetched the letter and the little bag from her basket and handed them both to the grandfather.

"I think that belongs to you," he declared, laying the little leather bag beside him on the bench. Then he read the letter and without a word put it into his pocket.

"Do you think you could still drink milk with me?" he asked Heidi and took her hand to go into the hut. "But take your money! You can buy a proper bed with it and enough clothes to last several years."

"I don't need it, Grandfather," assured Heidi. "I have got a bed already and Clara packed such a lot of clothes in my trunk that I shall never have to buy any ever again. It's wonderful."

"Take the money and put it into the cupboard, then. Some day you will want it."

Heidi obeyed and followed the grandfather into the hut. Joyfully she ran about and looked into every corner. Then she went up the ladder, but she stopped short when she put her head into the loft. "Oh, Grandfather, where is my bed?" she cried reproachfully.

"It will soon be there again," came from below. "How was I to know you were coming back? Come down and drink your milk."

Heidi came down and took her old seat in the high chair. Eagerly she drank her milk as though nothing had ever tasted so delicious. Then she took a deep breath and declared, "There is nothing in the whole world so good as our milk, Grandfather!"

Suddenly a shrill whistle sounded. Quick as lightning Heidi rushed outside, and there were the goats, skipping and jumping down the steep heights with Peter in their midst. Speechlessly he stared at Heidi.

"Good evening, Peter!" she said. "Do you still know me?"

The little goats had evidently recognised her voice, for they rubbed their heads against her eagerly. Heidi was wild with joy to see her old companions once more and called each one by name as they came scampering and leaping down to her. Even shy little Snowflake pushed the Great Turk out of her way in such a sure manner that he was left standing looking very put out by her bravado.

Heidi was thrilled to be back with all her old friends. She threw her arms around Snowflake's neck, stroked Goldfinch, and was pushed and nuzzled on all sides.

Slowly Peter came towards her. "So you are back again!" he managed to say at last. Then, just as in the old days, he asked, "Will you come up to the pasture, to-morrow?"

"No, not to-morrow, but the next day. To-morrow I must go and see the grandmother as I have been worried about her."

"I am glad you are back!" Peter said, beaming with happiness, and began to urge the goats down the mountain.

When Heidi got back into the cottage her bed was already made up for her. With a sigh of contentment she lay down and slept as she had not done for a whole year. During the night the grandfather got up again and again and listened anxiously to hear if Heidi slept quietly. But Heidi never stirred. Now there was nothing to make her wander about in the night-time for her longing was satisfied. She had seen the mountains again and had heard the wind in the fir trees. She was home on the Alm.

CHAPTER 14

The Bells Ring Out

Heidi stood under the fir trees and waited for the Alm-Uncle who was going to take her as far as the grandmother's and then go on to Dörfli to fetch her trunk. She was impatient to hear how the grandmother had enjoyed the white rolls and thought the grandfather would never be finished with his tasks, but at the same time she could not listen enough to the whispering of the trees, or breathe in the beautiful flower-filled air of the pastures. At last the old man appeared and announced, "Well, I have finished."

It was a Saturday, which was Alm-Uncle's day for cleaning and tidying the house. He had spent the morning doing this so that he could go with Heidi in the afternoon, and the hut was now shining bright and clean.

At Goat Peter's cottage they parted and Heidi ran inside. The grandmother heard her step and called lovingly, "Are you there, child? Have you come back again?" She took Heidi's hand and told her how much she had enjoyed the rolls and how much stronger she felt already. Brigitta explained how the grandmother would only take one roll each day for fear they would be finished too soon. At that Heidi exclaimed, "I know what I shall do, Grandmother. I shall write to Clara and I am sure she will send as many rolls as you want."

"That is very good of you," said Brigitta, "but I am afraid they would get very hard and stale. If only I had money! The baker in Dörfli makes them too, but I can't afford to buy them. I have hardly enough money for the ordinary black bread."

"Oh, but I have lots of money!" the child cried delightedly. "Now I know how I shall spend it. Every day Grandmother will have a white roll and two on Sundays and Peter will get them in Dörfli."

"No, no, my child," remonstrated the grandmother. "The money you have got is not for that; you must give it to the grandfather and he will tell you what to do with it."

But Heidi took no notice and continued to chatter happily, "Now Grandmother can eat a roll every day and will get quite strong. Perhaps it's only dark for you because you are so weak, Grandmother."

The grandmother said nothing. She did not want to spoil the child's joy.

Suddenly Heidi caught sight of the grandmother's hymn book and a new thought struck her:

"Grandmother, I can read now. Shall I read to you one of the hymns from your old book?"

"Yes, indeed," replied the grandmother, both surprised and delighted. "But do you really know how to read, child?"

Heidi had climbed on a chair and lifted down the dusty book which had lain untouched on the shelf for a very long time.

She blew the dust off and then sat down on the stool beside the old woman, asking which hymn she wanted to hear.

"Whichever you like, child! Whichever you like!" And she waited in eager expectation while Heidi turned over the pages and read softly a line here and there.

"Here is one about the sun. I shall read that one, Grandmother."

And Heidi read the hymn aloud, very touchingly.

The grandmother sat with folded hands while Heidi read and the face of the aged woman shone with an indescribable joy such as Heidi had never seen before, and her eyes glistened with tears. When the child stopped reading, "Once more, Heidi, please. Read it once more," she begged, and Heidi read the hymn again.

> The morning breaks,
> And warm and bright
> The earth lies still
> In golden light—
> For Dawn has scattered the clouds of night.

> God's handiwork
> Is seen around
> Things great and small
> To his praise abound—
> Where are the signs of his love not found.

> All things must pass
> But God shall still
> His will fulfill—
> Sure and unshaken is His will.

His saving grace
Will never fail
Though grief and fear
The heart assail—
O'er life's wild seas he will prevail.

Joy shall be ours
In that garden blest,
Where after storm
We find our rest—
I wait in peace—God's time is best.

"Oh, Heidi, that is enough to fill my heart with light. How comforting the words are!"

As the grandmother spoke, there was a knock at the window and the grandfather stood outside, beckoning Heidi to come home. She went at once, but not without promising the grandmother that she would come again to-morrow. She was completely happy because she could make the grandmother's life cheerful again. It was an even greater source of happiness to her than the goats and the pasture.

Heidi had so much to tell the grandfather, particularly about the rolls. "Surely, Grandfather," she

said, "if Grandmother won't take the money you
will give me money from the bag so that I can give
it to Peter to buy the rolls every day!"

"What about a bed, Heidi?" asked the grandfather. "A proper bed for you would be nice and there
would still be plenty left over for the rolls?"

But Heidi gave him no peace and at last the old
man said, "The money is yours to do with as you
please. You will be able to buy rolls for the
Grandmother with it for many, many years."

Heidi was jubilant. "Oh, Grandfather, isn't
everything wonderful!" Then she became serious.
"If God had answered when I prayed to come here
at once, everything would have been different. I
would only have come for a short time and
Grandmother would only have got a few rolls and I
wouldn't have been able to read to her. But God
has thought it out much better than I ever could,
just as Grandmamma told me in Frankfurt.
Everything has turned out as she said. Oh, how glad
I am that God did not let me have my way! Now I
all always pray as Grandmamma taught me and if
God does not do what I ask I shall think at once, 'I
am sure it is just the same as at Frankfurt and God
knows a much better way.' So we will pray every

day, please, Grandfather, and we will never forget
Him so that He does not forget us."

"And if somebody does forget Him?" murmured
the grandfather.

"Oh, it will be the worse for him! Because then
God will forget *him*, and nobody will pity him
because he ran away from God who could have
helped him."

"That is true, Heidi. But how do you know?"

"From Grandmamma. She explained it all to me."

The grandfather walked on silently, then, lost in
his own thoughts. He said, "But nobody can go
back once he has forgotten God and God has
forgotten him for ever."

"Oh, no, Grandfather! It's possible to go back. I
know that, too, from Grandmamma, and it even
says so in the lovely story in my book, but you have
not read it yet. As soon as we are home you shall
hear what a beautiful story it is."

As soon as they reached the top of the hill Heidi
ran into the cottage to get her book and returned
presently with it under her arm. The grandfather,
busy with his own thoughts, was seated on the
bench. Heidi climbed up beside him and opened
her book at her favourite story.

Now Heidi began to read the story of the Prodigal Son who, although he had all he could wish for at home tending his father's flock, longed for wealth and riches, and asked for his share of his father's wealth so that he could go out into the world and be his own master. After he had foolishly spent all he had, he was obliged to work as a swine-herd with nothing to wear but rags and nothing to eat but the husks which the pigs left. Then he remembered his father and thought what an ungrateful son he had been, and he wept bitterly. So he decided, 'I shall go to my father and ask forgiveness and say to him, "I am not worthy to be called thy son; make me one of thy day labourers."' But when he was still a great distance from his father's house, his father recognised him and hastened forward—

"And what do you think happens now, Grandfather?" Heidi could not help stopping to ask. "Do you think the father is still angry and will say to him, 'Go away!' Listen now to what happens next!"

"And when the father saw him coming he had compassion on him and embraced him, and the son said, 'Father, I have sinned against Heaven and in thy sight and am not worthy to be called thy son.'

But his father said to his servants, 'Bring the best robe for him. Put a ring on his finger and bring shoes for his feet. And bring forth the fatted calf and kill it and let us eat and be merry, for this, my son, was dead and is alive again; he was lost and is found.'

"Isn't that a beautiful story, Grandfather?" asked Heidi when she saw that he was still absorbed in his thoughts.

"Yes, Heidi, the story is beautiful," answered the grandfather, his face still grave. So Heidi was silent for a while and looked at the pictures in her book. After a while she laid the book on his lap and said, "Look, Grandfather, he is so happy standing there," pointing to the figure of the prodigal son, who was standing by his father in new clothes, as one of the family.

A few hours later when Heidi had been asleep for a long time, the grandfather climbed up the ladder and put his lamp beside her bed so that its light fell on the sleeping child. She was lying with folded hands, as if she had fallen asleep saying her prayers. On her little face was an expression of peace and trust. For a long time the old man stood gazing at the child, then he folded his hands and half aloud he prayed with bent head, "Father, I have sinned against Heaven and in Thy sight and am not worthy to be called Thy son." As he spoke tears rolled down the old man's cheeks.

Early next morning the Alm-Uncle stood in front of his hut, smiling gently as he looked around him. It was a beautiful Sunday morning and he could hear the church bells ringing down in the valley. He went back into the hut and called up to the loft, "Get up, Heidi! Put on your nice frock for we are going to church together."

Heidi was soon dressed in her pretty Frankfurt clothes and came downstairs quickly, her curiosity aroused by this unusual summons from the Alm-Uncle; but great was her surprise when she caught a glimpse of him. "Oh, Grandfather, I have never seen you in this coat with the silver buttons. How nice you look in your Sunday coat!"

The old man smiled and said, "You too, in your pretty dress. Come along now!" He took Heidi's hand in his and they walked down the mountain together. The bells were ringing on every side and the sound of them filled the whole valley and rose up echoing among the mountains. As they descended, the peals sounded louder and richer and Heidi listened rapturously. "Listen, Grandfather! It is like a great festival."

When the grandfather and Heidi entered the church the singing had already begun so they sat down together at the back. But before the hymn was finished there was subdued whispering on all sides, "The Alm-Uncle, did you see the Alm-Uncle?"

Soon everybody knew that the Alm-Uncle was in church and the women, hardly able to believe, kept turning their heads to look. When the sermon began, everybody became more attentive and forgot, for the time being, about the uncle.

As soon as the service was finished the old uncle walked with the child in the direction of the pastor's house. Some of the people followed him curiously and when they saw him and the child go inside, they gathered in excited groups to discuss the extraordinary event, for they could not imagine what had brought the old man down from his mountain-top. It soon became evident that many of them were beginning to change their opinion of the old man. They had noticed what great care he took of the little one and surely, they thought, he cannot be so very wicked or he would be afraid to face the pastor.

Then the baker reminded them, "Didn't I tell you? What child would give up a wonderful home with the best life can offer to go back to a grandfather who had been unkind and of whom she is afraid?" And so a friendly feeling for the grandfather began to spread amongst the people and they waited patiently at the pastor's door as though to welcome back an old friend who had been gone a long time.

The uncle knocked at the door of the pastor's study and the pastor greeted him as though he had expected the old man. His appearance in church had not escaped the pastor's notice and he shook hands warmly. At first the Alm-Uncle could not find words, then, pulling himself together, he began, "Pastor, I have come to ask you to forget the words I spoke to you on the Alm and not to hold it against me that I was too obstinate to take your well-meant advice. I see now that you were right and I was wrong, so I am following your advice and I would like to take the house in Dörfli for the winter, for the cold season up there is not good for the child. She is too delicate. Of course, the people here do not trust me and I deserve no better."

The kind eyes of the pastor brightened with joy. Once more he grasped the old man's hand and said

with deep emotion, "Neighbour, I am sincerely
glad; and you will never have cause to regret
coming back to live amongst us. You will always be
welcome in my house and I hope to spend many a
pleasant winter evening with you for I value your
friendship. And we shall also find playmates for the
little one."

The pastor laid his hand affectionately on Heidi's
curly head, and taking her by the hand, accompanied them both to the door. When they stood
outside on the doorstep he bade them good-bye and
everybody noticed that the pastor shook hands with
the Alm-Uncle as if they were the best of friends.

As soon as the door closed the old man was
assailed by friendly greetings from every one, "How
nice to see you again, Uncle!" "It's good to see you
back, Uncle. I have been wanting to have a talk with
you for a long time." And when the Uncle told
them that he was going to live again in his old house
in Dörfli for the winter months, there was such a
chorus of joyful shouts that it seemed as though the
Alm-Uncle was the most popular person in Dörfli.
The farming people accompanied the old man and
the child far up the mountain path and when they
said farewell every one invited him to call next time

he was down. When they parted, the old man
followed them with his eyes and his face reflected
an inner light so that Heidi could not take her eyes
off him. "Grandfather," she said, "today you look
nicer every minute. I have never seen you like this
before."

"Do you think so?" asked the old man, smiling.
"You see, Heidi, I am so happy to-day. To be at
peace with God and man is good! God was good to
me when He sent you to the Alm."

When they arrived at Goat Peter's hut, the grandfather opened the door and they walked inside.

"Good morning, Grandmother!" he said. "I think
we will have to do some more patching before the
autumn winds come."

"Mercy!" exclaimed the grandmother. "That is
the uncle!" and her voice was both surprised and
pleased. "Now I can thank you for all you have
done for us, Uncle. God bless you! God bless you!"
And when he held her trembling hand she said, "If
I have ever hurt you, don't punish me by taking
Heidi away from me. Oh, you do not know what the
child means to me." And she held Heidi close to
her.

"Have no fear, Grandmother. I shall not punish

either you or myself. We shall all stay together now
and, if God wills it, for a long time."

Brigitta beckoned the Uncle into a corner, and
showed him the hat with the feathers, explaining
how it came to be there and insisting that she could
not take such a thing from a child. But the grandfather, glancing towards Heidi, replied that Brigitta
should indeed take the hat, as Heidi was free to
decide if she didn't want it.

Brigitta was thrilled. "It is worth more than ten
shillings," she said, displaying it for all to admire.
"And what changes for the good Heidi has brought
with her from Frankfurt. I've a good mind to send
Peter there for a while—I am sure it would benefit
him tremendously."

The grandfather's eyes twinkled. He thought it
would probably do Peter good, but he meant to wait
for the right moment to broach the subject to him.

At that moment, Peter himself rushed in noisily
and evidently in a great hurry. He held a letter in his
hand which was a rare enough occurrence to
account for his excitement. It was a letter for Heidi
which had been given to Peter at the post office in
Dörfli. Heidi opened her letter and read it aloud. It
was from Clara.

She told Heidi how dull it had been since she had gone and how, for this reason, she had persuaded her father to take her to Ragatz next autumn so that she might have a chance of seeing her again. Grandmamma wished to come too, for she also wished to visit Heidi and the grandfather on the Alm; and Grandmamma was sending some coffee so that the grandmother would not have to eat the rolls dry. And she was looking forward to visiting the grandmother herself if Heidi would take her.

There were so many questions to ask and so much to discuss after this news that even the grandfather did not notice how quickly time was passing. Everybody was happy about the news but, as the grandmother said, the greatest delight of all was to see an old friend return like old times. "Come again, soon, Uncle, and you, child, tomorrow!"

They both promised. But now it was time to leave. As in the morning the bells had greeted them, so now the peaceful evening chimes accompanied them on their way up to the sunny Alm cottage which shone with an air of Sunday calm in the red glow of the evening sky. But when Grandmamma arrives next autumn there will be even more surprises for Heidi and for the grandmother; for a proper bed will certainly be put up in the hay loft. If Grandmamma has anything to do with it, everything turns out very well.

CHAPTER 15

Preparations for a Journey

It was a sunny morning in September and the good doctor, who had been the cause of Heidi's going home, was on his way to the Sesemann's house. There was a look of great sadness on his face and he seemed to have aged considerably since the spring. The doctor had had an only daughter in whom, since the death of his wife, he had found his only happiness. A few months before, she had died and, ever since, all the doctor's brightness and cheerfulness had gone.

Sebastian opened the door with marked civility, for the doctor was not only the best friend of the master but also of his little daughter, and because of his warmth and kindness was beloved by everyone in the house.

"Everything all right?" he asked Sebastian in his pleasant voice as he preceded the servant upstairs.

"Ah, I am glad you are here!" exclaimed Herr Sesemann as he stepped forward to welcome his friend. "We must definitely discuss again this Swiss journey. Do you still stick by your decision in spite of the fact that Clara's health shows signs of improvement?"

"My dear Sesemann, what am I to think of you!" replied the doctor. "This is the third time to-day you have called me in to ask the same question."

"Yes, you are perfectly right and I cannot blame you for becoming impatient; but you must understand, my dear friend, how difficult it is for me to deny the child now, at the last minute, something which I promised her so faithfully and to which she has been looking forward for months. It is only the prospect of this journey ant the thought of seeing her friend again which has enabled Clara to suffer so patiently these last bad weeks and now, suddenly, I am to deprive the poor child of this joy. I simply cannot do it."

"Sesemann, it has to be done," replied the doctor firmly, and when he saw his friend silent and depressed he continued, "now think it out for yourself. For years Clara hasn't had such a bad summer as this last one. There can be no question of travelling without risk of the worst consequences. And after all, it is September, and although there is a chance that it is still fine up there, it may very easily be cold. The days are getting shorter and the journey from Ragatz to the Alm would take several hours as Clara would have to be carried up the mountain. In short, Sesemann, it is quite impossible. But I shall speak to her myself. She is a sensible child. If she is taken to Ragatz next May for very special care and if she is stronger she will enjoy the excursion up the mountain far more than now. Only with the greatest care and attention can she have a chance of recovery."

Herr Sesemann suddenly turned to the doctor and said bluntly: "Tell me honestly, Doctor: do you really think she may one day recover?"

The doctor shrugged. "I don't hold out much hope," he said quietly. "But think what I have to go through. You still have a loving child to watch for you and to be there when you arrive home. You do not return to a lonely house, and Clara is comfortable there too. Despite all the things she has to miss she has many things for which to be grateful. No,

my friend, you have not a great deal to be sorry
about."

Herr Sesemann rose and walked up and down
the room as was his habit when something occupied his mind.

Suddenly he tapped his friend on the shoulder.

"Doctor, I have a suggestion to make. You don't
look well and are not the same as you used to be.
You need a change and do you know what has
occurred to me? You should go and visit Heidi on
the Alm in our name."

This suggestion surprised the doctor very much
and he started to make objections, but Herr
Sesemann gave him no opportunity. He was so
enthusiastic about his new plan that he took his
friend by the arm and drew him into Clara's room.
Clara was always pleased to see the doctor, for he
nearly always had some funny story to tell her.
Recently he had been more serious, but Clara knew
why, and would have given anything to see him
lively and cheerful once more.

Herr Sesemann took Clara's hand in his and
began to talk about the Swiss journey and how he
himself had looked forward to it. He passed quickly
over the main point—that it was impossible now for

Clara to go—for he could not bear the thought of
the tears which would be bound to fall, and then
told her of his latest plan to persuade their good
friend, the doctor, to take this holiday.

Tears came into Clara's eyes although she tried
to hide them for her father's sake, but it was a great
disappointment to her to have to give up this journey which had been her only joy and comfort
during many lonely hours. She knew, however, that
her father would only deny her something which
would do her harm; so she swallowed her tears and

tuned her thoughts to the only remaining hope. She
took the doctor's hand and said imploringly:

"Please, doctor, go and see Heidi and then come
back and tell me what it is like there and how Heidi
is getting on; and the grandfather, and Peter and
the goats. I feel I know them all so well! And then
you can take to Heidi all the things I have for her,
and something for the grandmother. Please go,
doctor, and I'll take as much cod liver oil as you
like."

It may not have been this promise which altogether decided the doctor but he certainly replied
smilingly: "Then I suppose I must go, Clara, if we
are to see you grow plump and strong! And when
have you decided I am to start?"

"As soon as possible, doctor. To-morrow morning," replied Clara.

"She is quite right," interrupted her father. "The
weather is fine and it would be a pity to miss a
single day which you could enjoy on the Alm."

The doctor could not help laughing a little.
"Soon you'll reproach me for not being there
already, Sesemann. I see I shall have to make
haste."

But Clara still detained him. She had to give him

lots of messages for Heidi. She would send round the presents later on. The doctor promised to deliver them all faithfully and to bring back a full account of everything that happened.

The servants of a household have a strange capacity for knowing what is going on long before they are informed about it by the master. Tinette, having been rung for, went into Clara's room. Clara asked her to fill a box with the cakes normally served with coffee. Tinette picked it up, and swinging it carelessly, carried it out. "I wouldn't have bothered if I'd been you," she said cheekily as she went out. Sebastian, as he opened the front door for the doctor, said with his usual deference: "May I ask the doctor to give my regards to the little fräulein?"

"Ah, Sebastian," the doctor smiled, "you know already about my going?"

Sebastian looked embarrassed, "Well, I—not exactly—as a matter of fact—well, you see, I just happened to go into the dining-room when I heard the little fräulein's name mentioned, and then I thought—"

"I see! I see!" smiled the doctor. "Good-bye, Sebastian! I'll be sure to remember your message."

The doctor stepped across the threshold, and then jumped back again quickly. The doorway was blocked by Fräulein Rottenmeier returning from her walk which she had been prevented from concluding by the rough wind. It was a very gusty day and the wind blew out her skirts so that she looked like a ship in full sail. The doctor drew aside to let her pass, but the wind was so strong she was blown right into the doorway and, gasping for breath, crashed into the doctor. The poor lady was very much upset by this loss of dignity for she had a great admiration for the doctor, but he very quickly smoothed her down and told her of his plans, asking her in a most amiable voice to pack the parcel for Heidi in the way in which only she could do it. Then off he went.

Clara had expected that Fräulein Rottenmeier would make all sorts of objections to sending the many presents to Heidi, but she was mistaken. Fräulein Rottenmeier was in an exceptionally good temper and everything was laid out on a large table where Clara could watch it all being packed. This was not an easy task, for the presents were all of different shapes and size. There was the little warm coat with the hood which Clara had herself designed for Heidi, so that during the long, cold winter she could be warm enough to visit the grandmother whenever he wanted. Then came a thick warm shawl for the grandmother in which she could wrap herself up and not feel the draught from the cold wind and also a large cake as a change from the rolls. There was the large box full of cakes, also for the grandmother, as a change from bread when she had her coffee. Then there was a delicious sausage which Clara had at first meant for Peter as he never had anything to eat except bread and cheese, but had later decided to send to Brigitta, since there might be a danger of Peter eating it all himself, and Brigitta could be depended upon to divide it up between all of them for supper. There was a packet of tobacco for the grandfather who was so fond of his pipe, and last of all, there were a lot of mysterious little packages which Clara had especially enjoyed putting together, as they had been made up specially to be put in as individual surprises for Heidi.

At last the job was done and an imposing-looking parcel lay on the floor ready for transport. Fräulein Rottenmeier looked at it with a satisfied smile, pleased with her efforts at the art of packing. Clara gazed at it blissfully, imagining Heidi's squeals of delight when it arrived.

Fräulein Rottenmeier rang for Sebastian and with an energetic swing he lifted the parcel on to his shoulder and carried it off to be despatched at once to the doctor's house.

CHAPTER 16

A Visitor to the Alm

The morning sky was all aglow, shedding its light upon the mountains, and a fresh breeze stirred in the fir trees, swaying their ancient branches. Heidi opened her eyes, awakened by the sound of the wind in the trees, and jumping out of bed, dressed herself very quickly. When she came down the ladder, the grandfather was already standing outside and was looking at the sky to see what sort of weather it was going to be. Little pink clouds floated across the sky and gradually more and more blue patches appeared. The sun was just rising and touched the mountain tops with gold.

"Oh, how lovely!" cried Heidi. "Good morning, Grandfather!"

"Are you awake already?" he said, patting the

child's head. She ran off to listen to the fir trees, and with every new gust of wind which blew through their old branches, she thrilled with pleasure.

The grandfather went off to milk the goats and brought them out ready for their climb up to the pastures. There came the sound of Peter's whistle and presently Heidi was surrounded by the whole flock who were all bleating, nuzzling and rubbing against her so that she could hardly move. Little Bear pushed rather harder than he should, and was gently reproached by Heidi; whereupon Little Swan lifted her head daintily, as if to imply that she would not stoop to such behaviour. Heidi, meanwhile, had pushed her way through to where Snowflake was standing, for the little goat had tried to reach her and had been pushed aside by the others. Peter at last gave one more piercing blast on his whistle, and the goats moved off.

"Are you coming with us to-day?" he asked and it was clear from the tone of his voice that he was anxious for Heidi to accompany him.

"No, Peter, I can't come to-day," replied Heidi. "The friends from Frankfurt may arrive at any moment and I must be here when they come."

"That's what you always say," grumbled Peter. "And I shall go on saying it until they arrive," returned Heidi. "How could you think that I would not stay here to greet them?" "The uncle is always here. So I can't see that it matters," he muttered.

Just at that point the uncle himself called out, "What's wrong with the army to-day, it isn't on the move? Is it the General's fault or is it the troops'?"

Peter turned at once and cracked his whip in the air, and the goats, who knew the sound well, started off up the mountain with Peter trotting after them.

Since Heidi had come back she thought of all sorts of things to do about the house which had not occurred to her before. Every morning she made her bed carefully, then she went downstairs and tidied the kitchen. She put the chairs straight and anything which was lying about she put into the cupboard. Next she would get out a duster, and climbing on to a chair, would rub the table until it shone. All this pleased the grandfather and he would look round, saying, "The house is so well kept nowadays it always looks as though it were Sunday! Heidi's trip certainly hasn't been in vain!"

To-day Heidi had begun her chores as usual but
the beautiful weather seemed to draw her outside
and she was not making much progress with her
work. A sunbeam slanting through the open
window seemed to be calling: "Come, Heidi! Come
out!" She simply could not stay indoors any longer
and ran outside. The sunlight sparkled on the
mountains and shone down on the valley. Heidi
had to sit down for a minute and look about her.
However, she soon jumped up and ran back to the
hut when she remembered that her stool was still
standing in the middle of the floor and that the
table had still not been rubbed properly.

Hardly had she set about her tasks again when
she heard the fir trees calling her and off she ran
again to listen to their song. The grandfather was
working in the shed and came out from time to
time to look smilingly at the child. He had just
gone back to his work when Heidi called out
loudly, "Grandfather! Grandfather! Come
quickly!" The old man came out at once, afraid
that something had happened to the child. He saw
Heidi running towards the path, calling as she
went, "They are coming! They are coming! The
doctor is first!"

Heidi rushed forward to welcome her old friend who stretched out his hand in greeting. As soon as she reached him she clasped his out-stretched arm affectionately. "Good morning, doctor, and thank you, ever so much, I am so grateful to you."

"God bless you, Heidi! And what is it you are grateful to me for?"

"For arranging it so that I could come home to be with grandfather," explained the child.

The doctor's face brightened with joy. He had not expected such a welcome. He had climbed the steep mountain path feeling lonely and depressed and with never a thought for the beautiful scenery around him. Convinced that Heidi would hardly even recognise him again he had pictured the disap-pointment his arrival without the expected friends would cause. But instead, here was Heidi beaming with joy and full of love and gratitude, and still clinging to his arm.

With fatherly tenderness the doctor took the child by the hand. "Take me to your grandfather, Heidi, and show me where you live."

But Heidi did not go on. Her gaze was fixed on the path down the mountain and her little face showed disappointment. "Where are Clara and Grandmamma?" she asked.

"I have something to tell you, Heidi, and I know you will be as sorry about it as I am," replied the doctor. "You see, Heidi, I have come alone. Clara has been very ill and could not travel, so the grandmamma did not come either. But in the spring, when the days begin to get warmer and longer, they will certainly come."

Heidi looked perplexed. It was difficult for her to realise that everything she had looked forward to was not to be. She stood frozen for a moment, overwhelmed by the sudden disappointment. The doctor stood silently before her and there was no sound save the sighing of the wind in the fir trees. Then it occurred to Heidi that after all the doctor had come and she looked up at him. The eyes that looked down into hers were sad. Heidi had never seen him look like this in Frankfurt and her heart was at once full of sorrow for him. No doubt, she decided, it was because Clara and the grandmamma could not come and she tried to think quickly of a way to comfort him.

"Oh, it won't be long until the spring and then they'll be sure to come, won't they?" she asked.

"The winter is never very long here, and when they do come, they will be able to stay much longer. Clara will certainly like that! Now let's go up to the grandfather."

Hand in hand with the doctor, she climbed up to the cottage and called out cheerfully to the grandfather. "They haven't come yet, but it won't be long."

The doctor was no stranger to the grandfather, for Heidi had talked about him a great deal. The old man welcomed his guest heartily and then the two men sat down on the bench before the cottage and there was still a little place for Heidi beside the doctor. The doctor started to explain:

"Herr Sesemann wanted me to come and I allowed myself to be persuaded because I have not been well for quite a time and I thought the fresh mountain air would do me good. Heidi," said the doctor, stooping towards her, "there will be something coming up here which has travelled with me all the way from Frankfurt—something which will give you more pleasure than the old doctor."

Heidi was intensely interested to know what it could be but the doctor would not give a hint.

The grandfather encouraged the doctor to spend the beautiful autumn days on the Alm, or at least, to come up every fine day. "I cannot invite you to stay here, as I have no accommodation, but if you would take a room down in Dörfli in the pleasant little inn instead of going back to Ragatz you could come up here in the mornings. There are many places round about which I would take pleasure in showing you."

This proposal delighted the doctor and so it was settled.

Time had passed quickly and it was now noon. The wind had dropped and the fir trees were quiet in the sun. The air was beautifully clean up there, but was nevertheless warm and gentle with its fill of sunlight. The Alm-Uncle rose and went into the cottage and brought back a little table which he placed in front of the bench. "Now, Heidi. Fetch everything we need for the meal," he ordered. "The doctor has to be content with our simple fare but he must admit that the dining-room is very pleasant."

"It is, indeed," agreed the doctor, looking down into the sunlit valley, "I gladly accept your kind invitation. Everything is bound to taste good in such surroundings."

Heidi ran to and fro like a busy little squirrel and brought whatever she could find in the cupboard for she wanted to show her pleasure in being able to entertain the doctor. The grandfather prepared the meal and appeared presently with the steaming milk jug and golden-brown toasted cheese. From the meat which he had cured himself he cut nice thin slices and the doctor ate more heartily than he had done for a whole year.

"Yes, Clara must certainly come here," he said. "It will give her new strength, and if her appetite is as good as mine has been to-day she'll grow plump and strong in no time."

As the doctor spoke, a man appeared coming up the path with a big bundle on his back. Panting, he arrived at the hut and put it down with a sigh of relief. "This is what I have brought with me all the way from Frankfurt," said the doctor, rising. The bundle was opened and when the first wrapping had been taken off he said: "Now, child, you go on and get out the treasure for yourself."

Heidi looked with big, astonished eyes at each item as it was unwrapped, speechless with pleasure.

The doctor lifted the lid of one of the boxes. "Look, Heidi. Something the grandmother can have with her coffee!"

Heidi picked up the cake and skipped around with it joyfully: "Oh, a cake for the grandmother!" Heidi wanted to go down at once to the grandmother with the presents, but the grandfather persuaded her to wait until the evening when she could accompany the doctor on his way down and take the presents at the same time.

Now Heidi found the packet of tobacco and handed it to the grandfather who started at once to fill his pipe. The two men went back and sat down on the bench, leaving Heidi to continue her inspection of Clara's parcel alone. After she had admired them all sufficiently, Heidi put away the many presents and came back to where the men were sitting. As soon as there was a gap in the conversation she addressed their guest very solemnly:

"No, the parcel did not give me as much pleasure as your visit, doctor."

The two men could not help laughing at her childish gravity.

As the sun set behind the mountains, the guest rose to take his leave and begin his walk down to Dörfli. The grandfather took the presents under his arm, the box with the cake, the big sausage and the shawl; the doctor took Heidi's hand and so all three walked down to Goat Peter's cottage where Heidi was to wait for her grandfather, who would first accompany their guest into Dörfli. Here Heidi said good night to the doctor and asked: "Would you like to come with the goats to-morrow?"

"Very well, Heidi. We'll go together," he replied. Now the two men walked on down the valley and Heidi ran into the cottage; taking first the cake box, then bringing in the big sausage, and last of all the shawl. She put everything very close to the grandmother so that the old woman would be able to touch the presents; and she laid the shawl on her knees.

"It has all come from Clara and the grandmamma in Frankfurt," she told the astonished Brigitta and the grandmother, Brigitta watching in amazement as one heavy package after another was dragged through the door.

"Aren't you delighted with the cake,

Grandmother?" Heidi wanted to know again and
again.

"Yes, Heidi. What kind people they must be!"
Then she felt the warm, soft shawl and said, "How
cosy it will be in the winter-time! I never dreamt I
would possess anything so luxurious."

Heidi was surprised that the grandmother was
more pleased about the shawl than the cake.

Brigitta was gazing at the sausage with a look in
her eyes little short of worship. Never in her life had
she seen such an enormous sausage, and she had
certainly never owned one. She shook her head and
looking puzzled, said, "I still have to ask Uncle
what we should do with it."

But Heidi replied straight away, "You must eat it!
That's what it's for."

Then Peter came rushing in. "The Alm-Uncle is
just behind me, Heidi—" Peter stopped and gasped
with astonishment as he caught sight of the sausage.
Heidi understood immediately that she must leave,
for it was getting late and although the grandfather
always stopped by nowadays to greet the old lady,
they would have a dark climb to the hut tonight.
The grandfather never let Heidi go to bed too late,
for she was always up at sunrise, so on this occasion

he wished everyone goodnight through the open door, and started back with Heidi straight away, climbing to their peaceful home under a star-filled sky.

CHAPTER 17

A Compensation

Early next morning the doctor climbed up to the Alm with Peter and the goats. The man and the boy walked in silence. In vain the kindly doctor had tried to start up a conversation with the boy but Peter remained obstinately silent and would not be coaxed into chatting about himself. Up at the Alm cottage Heidi waited with her two goats looking as sunny and sparkling as the morning.

"Are you coming?" asked Peter as he did every morning.

"Of course, if the doctor is coming, too," replied Heidi.

Peter cast a suspicious glance at the gentleman.

The Alm-Uncle came out of the hut carrying the lunch bag which he flung across Peter's shoulder. It was heavier than usual, for the uncle had put in something extra for the doctor in case he decided to stay long enough on the pasture to have his lunch with the children. When Peter felt the extra weight a grin spread across his face and the sulky look vanished. His thoughts were busy with the special tit-bits which the uncle might have put in the bag.

Now the trip started. The goats came crowding round Heidi as usual, so that she could hardly move forward, and eventually she stopped and told them to go on ahead properly and behave themselves. Gradually she was able to push them on in front of her, leaving her space to walk with the doctor, who took her by the hand. He had no difficulty this time in making conversation, for Heidi had so much to say about the goats, the mountains, the flowers and the birds, that time passed quickly and they soon found themselves at the pasture. All the way up Peter had cast hostile glances at the doctor, which had fortunately gone unnoticed by Heidi and her companion. Heidi led the doctor to her favourite spot where she liked to sit, and the doctor sat down on the grass beside her, casting a contented glance around him at the wide, green, sunlit valley. The snowfield glittered in the clear autumn sunlight, and the two rocky peaks were sharply silhouetted against the deep blue sky. A gentle breeze blew across the valley, gently ruffling the late summer flowers which still waved amongst the grasses. The eagle flew silently above them. Heidi looked around her with delight. Everything was so perfect. Her eyes sparkled with happiness and she glanced round at her friend to see if he too was enchanted with the beautiful scenery. The doctor had been sitting, silent and thoughtful, but when he met Heidi's eager, inquiring eyes, he said, "Yes, Heidi, it is beautiful, but if one's heart is sad how is it possible to enjoy all this beauty? Can you tell me?"

"Oh!" Heidi exclaimed confidently. "No one is ever sad here. That only happens in Frankfurt."

The doctor smiled quietly, then he asked again, "But if somebody brings all the sadness from Frankfurt up here, Heidi, do you know what to do then?"

"When we don't know what to do we have only to tell God about our troubles," said Heidi seriously.

"Well, my dear, that seems to be a good idea," remarked the doctor, "but what if God Himself has sent the sorrow? What can one say to Him, then?"

Heidi had to think about this. "Then, we must wait," she said, "and just keep thinking, 'soon God will make things right.' We have only to have a little patience and not run away; then something will turn up and we will see quite clearly that all the time it was all for the bet. At the time we only think of the sadness."

"You have a wonderful faith, Heidi, and you must never lose it." The doctor was silent, gazing at the towering mountains above them. Then he said again, "You see, Heidi, when someone has a great grief he cannot enjoy anything lovely, and beauty, like this around us, only makes him more sad. Can you understand that?"

Heidi thought sadly of the old grandmother who would never see again the splendour of the sun and the mountains. Every time she thought about darkness Heidi sorrowed anew for the grandmother, and for a while she said nothing. Then, "Yes, I can understand that." Then she said softly, "That's how it was with the grandmother until I read the hymns for her from the old book. She says they made everything light for her again and made her happy."

"Can you remember any of the hymns, Heidi?" asked the doctor.

"Yes, shall I say one to you?" replied Heidi eagerly.

The doctor nodded, and Heidi folded her hands and started to recite the grandmother's favourite hymn.

> Let not your heart be troubled
> Nor fear your soul dismay,
> There is a wise Defender
> And he will be your stay.
> Where you have failed, he conquers,
> See, how the foeman flies
> And all your tribulation
> Is turned to glad surprise.
>
> If for awhile it seemeth
> His mercy is withdrawn,
> That he no longer careth
> For his wandering child forlorn,
> Doubt not His great compassion,
> His love can never tire,
> To those who wait in patience
> He gives their heart's desire.

She stopped. The doctor did not look as though he were listening. He was sitting quite still, with his

hand over his eyes. Heidi thought he had perhaps
fallen asleep. But he was wide awake, and thinking
about a very long time ago, when he had been a
little boy, and his mother had read him the very
same hymn. He could see his mother's loving gaze
and hear her dear voice, and she seemed to be
saying many things to him. It was some while
before he stirred, to see Heidi looking at him in a
puzzled way.

"That was a beautiful hymn, Heidi," he said. "I
would like you to read it to me again next time we
come here together."

All this time Peter had been standing apart and
growing more and more angry because the old
gentleman sat beside Heidi all the time so that Peter
had not once had a chance to speak to her. He felt
so cross, he stood behind the doctor and shook his
fist at him. Peter knew by the sun that it was
midday and time for lunch, so he called out at the
top of his voice, "Dinnertime!"

Heidi got up to bring the rucksack to where they
sat, but the doctor said he was not hungry and only
wanted a glass of milk and wanted to climb higher.
Heidi did not feel very hungry either and she
wanted to take the doctor to the spot where

Greenfinch had nearly jumped to her death, so she ran to Peter and asked him to fetch two bowls of milk, one for the doctor and one for herself. Peter looked at her in surprise and asked, "What about all the food in the rucksack?"

"You can have it, Peter," replied Heidi, "but bring the milk first."

Peter had never been so quick in all his life and when he opened the rucksack and saw all the good food he was ashamed of making such faces at the doctor's back. So he ran to where he had stood shaking his fist at the doctor. There he held up his unclenched hands to show that he no longer bore any ill-will, then raced back down to his enormous meal, knowing his conscience was clear.

Heidi and the doctor wandered about together and talked for a long time until the doctor decided it was time for him to go home. Heidi accompanied him down the mountain as far as the Alm-hut. She held his hand all the way and chattered to him about the joys of life on the mountain, where the most beautiful flowers grew and so on. Heidi could name every Alpine flower growing, for her grandfather had taught her well.

At last the doctor insisted on Heidi's returning to the hut, and then he went on alone, turning now and again to see Heidi still standing on the same spot and waving to him just as his own little daughter might have done.

The month remained beautiful throughout. The doctor came up to the Alm every morning and sometimes went out with the Alm-Uncle whose conversation he enjoyed very much, for the old man knew the ways of all the wild animals and had many interesting stories to tell. He knew all kinds of uses for the plants on the mountainside, from the scented pines, to the curling moss which was found everywhere.

He also had marvellous tales to relate of the animals living in holes, caves and trees all over the mountain.

And so the lovely month of September passed. On the finest days, the doctor would climb the Alm with Heidi, and they would sit together whilst Heidi read hymns and talked of things which she had learnt from her life there.

Peter sat some way away from them, but was more or less resigned to the situation, and no longer flew into tantrums. One morning the doctor did not look quite so happy as usual and told them that this would be his last day and that he would have to return to Frankfurt. "I am very sad to go," he admitted, "for I feel now as if the Alm were my home."

The Alm-Uncle was sorry to hear this news of the doctor's departure for he too had enjoyed his companionship. Heidi could hardly believe that her dear friend had to go and she looked at him beseechingly; but the doctor's smile told her that his visit was at an end. She accompanied him a little of the way until the doctor stopped and said lovingly, stroking her curly hair, "Heidi, I have to go away now. How I would love to take you with me to Frankfurt!"

Heidi recalled Frankfurt, with its many houses and long streets. She remembered Fräulein Rottenmeier and Tinette and replied despondently, "I would rather you came back to us."

"You are right. That will be better," said the doctor. "Good-bye, then, Heidi." His kind eyes looked down on her for an instant and then he turned away quickly and continued his walk down the valley.

Heidi did not move. The sight of tears in the

doctor's eyes had upset her and suddenly she started to cry. Then she ran after the doctor as fast as she could, and as soon as she was beside him she sobbed, "I want to come with you! Just let me go back and tell Grandfather!"

The doctor tried to soothe the excited child. "Oh, my dear Heidi," he comforted her, "you must stay here among the fir trees or you may become ill again. But you can promise me this: if I should ever become ill and lonely would you come then and stay with me? If I could know that there would be someone to care for me then."

"Oh, yes, I would come at once. I love you nearly as much as the grandfather."

Once again the doctor said farewell and Heidi stood and waved as long as he remained in sight. As he turned for the last time he whispered to himself, "It is good to live up there. One is restored, body and soul, and knows again what it is to be happy."

CHAPTER 18

Winter in Dörfli

Snow lay high around the Alm cottage until the windows appeared to be level with the ground. If the Alm-Uncle had still been living there he would have to have done the same as Peter did every day. When snow had fallen during the night Peter had to jump out of the window, and if there was no frost he sank so deeply into the snow that he had to struggle with both hands and feet to get out again. Then his mother would hand him a shovel and he would scrape a path to the door. He had to dig the snow well clear of the house, otherwise the pile of snow would fall inside as soon as the door was opened. But if there was severe frost the house was shut in altogether except for the little window through which only Peter was able to creep. But the great advantage of the frost was that once Peter got through the little window he would be on hard, frozen snow. His mother would hand him his little sleigh through the window and Peter would go where he pleased, for the whole Alm was one huge sledging track.

The Alm-Uncle had kept his word. As soon as the first snows began to fall he had shut up the cottage and the shed and had taken Heidi and the goats down to Dörfli to live. Near the church stood a building which had, once upon a time, been a mansion house. A famous soldier had once lived there; he had been cited for bravery whilst fighting in Spain and had returned home much the richer. On his return he used some of his money to build a beautiful house where he intended to live.

But rural life was too quiet for him, and it was not long before he left again, this time never to return. After many years a relative took over the house, being certain that the soldier must have died. It was in such a poor state of repair that he did not wish to incur the expense of rebuilding it, so it was let for a nominal rent to the poor people of the district. Thus, if part of it fell down, it was not replaced. Although it was now half in ruins it still retained something of its former dignity. When the uncle had come to Dörfli with his son, Tobias, he had lived in this neglected house, and since that time it had been empty, for no one could live in it who did not know how to close up all the gaps and holes to keep out the wind which blew out the candle and made draughts all through the dilapidated old house.

But all this the uncle could fix, and when he had decided to spend the winter in Dörfli he had come down many times in the autumn to repair the house. Then, in October, he and Heidi had taken up their abode.

Entering from the back, one came first into a tumbledown building where, on one side, the wall had collapsed completely. Although the other wall was half in ruins the arch of an old window was still visible but thickly overgrown with ivy. The roof was vaulted and this had apparently been the chapel.

Next one entered a large hall where the walls and the ceiling had partly collapsed, and to prevent further ruin, strong pillars had been put in for support. Here the Alm-Uncle had built a partition and had covered the ground with straw, for this was to be the goat-house.

After going through many passages where in places the broken roof revealed patches of sky, one at last entered, through a heavy oak door, a spacious room which was still in good condition. The four strong walls with dark panelling were unbroken, and in one corner a stove reached to the ceiling. On white tiles big blue pictures were painted, representing old castles buried amidst high trees, huntsmen with their dogs or quiet lakes bordered by shady trees with a fisherman in the foreground. A bench was built all round the stove and here one could sit and study the pictures.

This attracted Heidi at once, and as soon as they entered the room she ran to the stove, sat down on the bench and began to look at the pictures. But as she slid along and round towards the back of the stove she found something else to attract her attention. Between stove and wall four boards had been put up. It might have been a place for storing apples but there were no apples there now and it was, quite obviously, going to be Heidi's bed just like the one on the Alm; a high straw bed with a sheet on it and the sack as a cover. Heidi was overjoyed. "Oh, Grandfather! This is going to be my room. How nice! But where are you going to sleep?"

"Your room has to be near the stove to keep you warm," declared the grandfather. "But you shall see mine, too."

Heidi ran through the huge room behind the grandfather who opened a door on the other side. This led into a small room where the old man had made up his bed. Then there was another door, and Heidi stood amazed when she looked into the spacious kitchen. In this room there were many signs of the grandfather's activity but there still remained a great deal of work to be done to fill up all the holes and crannies through which the wind still whistled. He had already made the old door strong, with the judicious use of screws and nails, and it served well as protection against the elements and the numerous insects which lived in the weeds surrounding the building.

Heidi was delighted with their new home, and the next day when Peter came she showed him all over the house, for she had already explored every corner. She insisted that he inspect each and every thing to be found in it, before he went.

Heidi slept comfortably and well in her warm corner, but every time she woke she thought immediately of the mountain and had to restrain herself from the impulse to rush outside and see why the trees were so quiet. She had to remind herself of her surroundings, and occasionally felt uneasy when she realised that she was not in her real home. But then the comforting sound of her grandfather's voice, and the bleating of the goats would reassure her, and once again Heidi was happy, and would leap out of bed and run to join the animals as quickly as she could.

Four days after they had settled down Heidi announced to the grandfather one morning that she must go and visit the grandmother. "I can't leave her alone any longer," she said. But the grandfather would not agree.

"Not to-day or to-morrow," he said. "The Alm is covered fathom-deep in snow, and it is still falling; Peter can hardly get through. A little one like you would soon be buried and no one would be able to find you. Wait a little until it freezes and then you can walk up quite comfortably."

At first Heidi was impatient at the thought of having to wait, but the days were busy and passed quickly. Every morning and afternoon she went to school and learned eagerly. She hardly ever saw Peter there for he seldom turned up. The teacher was a kind man and would remark tolerantly, "Peter absent to-day again! Ah, well, the snow is lying high, he won't be able to get through."

But in the evening, when school was finished, Peter always seemed able to come down to see Heidi no matter how deep the snow! After a few days the sun came out again and shone strongly on the wintry landscape, but the days were short and at night the moon would take up the vigil, clear and huge and sparkling, so that the whole mountain glittered.

One morning, when Peter, as usual sprang from the window into the snow he found that it had hardened with the strong frost of the previous night. The hard ice came as a surprise to him and he could not stop himself sliding off down the Alm which was frozen over as hard as iron. This delighted Peter because he knew that Heidi would be able to come up now to the cottage. Quickly he rushed back to the house and hurriedly swallowing his breakfast he announced, "I must be off to school!"

"Yes, go and learn as much as you can," said his mother.

Peter climbed through the little window, got on to his sledge and went shooting rapidly down the mountain. He went so fast that when he reached Dörfli he was quite unable to stop and the sledge skimmed along until it reached level ground when it stopped of its own accord. Peter got up and looked about. The headlong drive had taken him some way beyond Mayenfeld. It would take him an hour to climb up again and that would be much too late for school, thought Peter, so he might as well take his time. He arrived back in Dörfli just as Heidi and the grandfather were sitting down to dinner. Peter entered and as he had something special to tell them to-day he began right away.

"It's done it!" he fairly shouted.

"Eh! What has?" asked the old man. "You sound quite warlike to-day, General."

"The snow—frozen!" announced Peter.

"Oh, now I can go to the grandmother!" rejoiced Heidi, who was quick to understand Peter's odd way of expressing himself. "But why didn't you come to school? You could easily have come on the sledge," she added reproachfully, for she felt that it was not the thing to do to stay away if it were possible to attend.

"Took me too far down," said Peter. "So it was too late."

"Now that's what I'd call desertion," said the uncle, "and people who do that get their ears pulled; do you hear?"

Peter fidgeted uncomfortably, for there was no one whom he feared and respected more than the Alm-Uncle.

"And a leader like you should be doubly ashamed of himself," continued the uncle. "What would you do if your goats ran anywhere they liked?"

"Beat them," Peter replied smartly.

"And if a boy behaved like that and got a good beating, what would you say then?"

"Serves him right," was the answer.

"Very well, then, if it should happen again that your sledge passes the school when you should be inside, come to me and get what you deserve!"

At last the meaning of the uncle's little speech was beginning to dawn on Peter. He looked quite thunderstruck and retreated into a corner looking round in a frightened way in case there should be a stick in sight similar to the one he sometimes used on the goats. But the uncle said cheerfully, "Come now and eat with us and then Heidi can go up with you. In the evening you can bring her home again and have your supper here."

This unexpected turn to the conversation cheered Peter immensely. He obeyed at once and sat beside Heidi, who could hardly eat for excitement about going to the grandmother's. She pushed aside her plate of potatoes and toasted cheese, and offered it to Peter, together with the helping which the Uncle was already giving him. He was not put off, however, by the enormous amount of food on his p!ate, and started eating heartily straight away.

Heidi ran to the cupboard and brought out the little warm coat with the hood which Clara had given her. Putting it on she stood waiting beside Peter and as soon as he had swallowed his last bite she said, "Come along now!" On the way, Heidi told Peter how unhappy the two goats had been at first in their new surroundings, and how they would not eat nor make any sound. She had asked her grandfather why this was so, and he told her that they were feeling as she had.

When they arrived at the cottage, Peter's mother was alone in the room. She told them that the grandmother was not very well and had had to stay in bed because it was so cold. Heidi had always been accustomed to seeing the grandmother in her place in the corner. She ran to the other room and there lay the old woman in her narrow bed with only a thin coverlet over her, but wrapped in the warm grey shawl . . . .

"Thank God!" exclaimed the old woman when she heard Heidi running in, for she had had a secret fear that the gentleman from Frankfurt, with whom Heidi had been seen out walking on the Alm, would take the child away.

"Are you very ill, Grandmother?" asked Heidi with concern.

"No, no, child!" said the old woman and patted Heidi lovingly. "It is only the frost getting into my bones a little."

"Will you be better as soon as it is warm again?" Heidi persisted.

"Yes, yes, and with God's help before that so that I can get back to my spinning," said the grandmother, noticing how worried the child was.

This cheered Heidi a little, for she had never seen the grandmother ill in bed before, and was greatly upset. "Grandmother, in Frankfurt people put on a shawl when they go for a walk. Did you think it was for going to bed?" she said thoughtfully.

"I have put the shawl on in bed to keep warm, Heidi. You see the cover is rather thin."

"But, Grandmother," Heidi started again, "your pillow goes downhill instead of uphill!"

"Yes, I know, child." The grandmother tried to find a more comfortable place on the thin pillow which looked as hard as a board. "You see, the pillow has never been particularly soft and now I have slept on it for so many years that it has become quite flat."

"If only I had asked Clara if I could take my bed home! I had three big, thick pillows and they were so high I could hardly sleep for my head slipping off them. Could you have slept on them, Grandmother?"

"I am sure I could. One keeps warmer that way and breathes more easily when the head is high. However, don't let's speak about it. I have so much for which to thank God. The nice rolls I get, and the lovely warm shawl, and you coming to see me, Heidi. Would you care to read some of my favourite hymns to me to-day?"

Heidi got down the old hymn book and chose the most beautiful verses for they were all familiar to her now and she was as pleased as the old lady to

hear them again. As the grandmother listened, a
joyous smile lightened her face which had looked so
worn and tired before.

Heidi stopped. "Grandmother, are you feeling
better already?" she asked.

"Yes, child, I am much better already. Please
read to the end." Heidi read the last lines:—

"As the eyes grow dim, and darkness
Closes round, the soul grows clearer,
Sees the goal to which it travels,
Gladly feels its home is nearer."

As she read them, the grandmother repeated the
words softly to herself, with a serene expression on
her face. Heidi remembered the beautiful day of her
return home and her face lit up with joy.

"Grandmother, I know just what it means to be
going home."

The grandmother made no reply but the happy
expression stayed on her face.

After a while the child said: "I must go home
now, Grandmother. It is getting late. I am so glad
you are feeling better." The grandmother held
Heidi's hand.

"I feel at peace again, even if I have to stay here.
It is dreadful to have to lie alone for days on end,

without light or sound. It makes me sad and I sometimes feel that it is too much for me to stand. But to hear you read the hymns to me gives me comfort and peace in my heart once more."

Heidi said good-bye to the grandmother and she and Peter set off quickly, for the darkness was already coming down. As Peter got out his sledge the moon came through and shone brightly on the white snow so that it seemed as if the day were about to break. Peter sat in front, and off they shot down the Alm like two birds.

That night, as Heidi lay in her warm bed behind the stove, she thought about the grandmother and how she would like to visit her every day, for if she could read to her more often, perhaps the peace and light which came to her would help make her better. But Heidi knew one or two weeks might pass before she was allowed to go up again. She thought and thought about how things could be arranged. Suddenly she had an idea and she could hardly wait for daylight to carry out her plan. She suddenly sat upright in bed, for she had been so busy thinking about her plan that in her excitement she had forgotten to say her prayers.

When she had prayed from the bottom of her

heart for the grandfather and the grandmother and all the people she knew, she lay down on the soft hay and slept soundly and peacefully until the morning.

CHAPTER 19

Winter Continues

Next morning, Peter turned up at school in good time. He had brought his lunch with him, as did all the children who lived any distance from the school. They all sat at tables at mid-day and with their lunches on their knees and their feet upon the benches, ate heartily, whilst the other children went home to Dörfli.

They were free to do whatever they liked until one o'clock, when school recommenced. As was his usual habit when he happened to be at school, Peter paid a visit afterwards to the uncle. To-day, immediately he entered the house, Heidi rushed to him. "Peter, I have thought of something!" she exclaimed.

"What is it?" he asked.

"You must learn to read now," was her reply.

"I know how to read—a little."

"Yes, yes, Peter, but I mean so well that you can read easily and quickly."

"I'll never be able to do that," remarked Peter gloomily.

"I don't believe that, and neither would anybody else," said Heidi with determination. "Grandmamma told me some time ago that I was not to believe you. I shall teach you. I know quite well how to do it. You must learn now, and then you will be able to read one or two hymns to Grandmother every day."

"Oh, I don't care about *that*!" Peter grumbled.

This obstinacy towards something which she considered was kind and right annoyed Heidi. With flashing eyes she stood before the boy and said threateningly, "Then I will tell you what will happen if you refuse to learn. Your mother has said already that she will send you to Frankfurt to be taught, and I have seen the building where the boys go to school. Clara showed it to me. But they don't go there just when they are boys, but always, even when they are grown up. And don't think there is only one teacher as in our school."

A cold shudder ran down Peter's back.

"And you will have to go there among all the teachers and pupils," Heidi continued, "and if you cannot even read, and make mistakes with your spelling, you'll see how much they will laugh at you; much worse than Tinette, and if you only knew what she was like!"

"All right, then. I will," said Peter reluctantly.

Heidi was mollified at once. "That's right. We can start to-day," she decided joyfully. She dragged Peter to the table and brought out the necessary books. In Clara's big parcel there had been a book which Heidi thought was just right for teaching Peter, for it was an A B C book with verses.

They both bent over the book and the lesson began. Peter had to spell out the first verse again and again for Heidi wanted him to be able to read it correctly and fluently. At last she said, "You still don't know the verse so I shall read it to you. If you know the meaning it will be easier for you to spell it." And Heidi read:

> "Learn A B C without a grudge
> Or you'll be brought before the judge."

"I won't," said Peter obstinately.

"What?" asked Heidi.

"Go before the judge," was the answer.

"Hurry up then and learn these three letters and you won't need to."

Peter started again and repeated the three letters until Heidi said, "Now you can read these three! And read them carefully!"

As she noticed the effect this verse had had upon Peter she thought it would be a good idea to prepare him a little for the following lessons.

"Wait! I'll read the other verses to you now,"

she continued, "and you'll see what else can happen."

And she began to read very slowly and clearly:

"D E F G must smoothly flow
Or you will get a nasty blow.

If you forget H I J K
The fatal blow will fall to-day.

To learn L M is not a strain
And will prevent a lot of pain.

Remember well N O P Q
Or you'll get what's in store for you.

R S T may save a smack
If you will make a quick attack."

Here Heidi stopped because Peter was so quiet. All these secret hints and threats had petrified him with fright and he stared anxiously at Heidi. Her kind heart was touched at once and she said reassuringly, "You don't need to be afraid, Peter. If you come every evening and learn as well as you have done to-day you will soon know the letters and nothing will happen to you. But you must come *every* day and not just sometimes as you did with school—even if it snows. The snow doesn't trouble you anyway."

Peter promised. Fear of punishment had made him quite docile. Then he set off home.

He followed Heidi's advice and arrived promptly every evening. The letters were studied with zeal and the verses taken to heart. Often the grandfather listened to the lessons while he contentedly smoked his pipe. Every now and then his face would twitch with amusement. Peter was usually asked to stay to supper with them which was a great compensation to him for the anxiety which the verses caused.

So the winter passed. Peter appeared regularly and made good progress. He had now got as far as U and Heidi read:

"Who still mistakes the U for V
May go where he won't like to be."

This gave Peter an uncomfortable feeling but made him learn all the quicker lest the threat were carried out. The following evening the verse was:

"If W is still unknown
The stick may come into its own."

Peter remarked sneeringly, "There isn't one."
But Heidi reminded him that the grandfather had
a very big stick in his cupboard, at least as thick as
Peter's arm and this made him bend over his W in
a feverish effort to memorise it. Next was:

"X is a cross you may recall
And this is easiest of them all."

And Heidi quickly prompted him to learn another
letter as well so that only the last one remained for
the following day. Although Peter tried to object,
Heidi read out:

"To stop at Y will never do
And all the world will laugh at you."

Peter at once attacked the Y with energy, imagining
the gentlemen of Frankfurt in their tall black hats,
jeering at him and scorning his inadequacy. He did
not give up until he could close his eyes and still
remember what it looked like.

Peter arrived the next day feeling very jaunty because there was only one more letter to be learnt and when Heidi read the verse:

> "Who still forgets the Z you know
> Straight to the Hottentots will go,"

he said sarcastically, "Who knows where they live?"

"Grandfather does. Wait! I shall ask him at once. He is only across the road with the pastor."

Heidi was about to run to the door when Peter exclaimed in alarm, "Wait a moment!" In his imagination he saw both the pastor and the uncle carrying him off and sending him away to the Hottentots—because he really had forgotten completely what Z was like.

"What is the matter?" Heidi asked in surprise.

"Nothing! Come back! I shall learn now," muttered Peter.

Heidi, though, wanted to know just where the Hottentots were to be found, and persisted in her suggestion that she should ask the grandfather, but Peter seemed so desperately anxious that she should not, that she eventually changed her mind. Instead, she made him repeat the letter until it was

engraved on his brain, and in addition she began to
teach him spelling, at which Peter made a very good
start indeed. And from day to day Peter made
progress with his reading.

The ice had thawed and new snow had fallen
every day so that about three weeks had passed
since Heidi's visit to the grandmother. This made
her work all the harder with Peter so that he would
be able to take her place and read to the old woman.

One evening Peter went home and announced, "I
can do it now!"

"What can you do, Peter?" asked his mother.

"Read," he answered.

"Did you hear that, Grandmother?" Brigitta
exclaimed.

Grandmother did hear and was wondering how
this had come about.

"I have to read a hymn now. Heidi said so."

Brigitta quickly fetched the book and the grandmother smiled in anticipation of hearing the
comforting words once more. Peter sat down and
began to read and his mother sat beside him, listening, and saying after each verse, in a voice full of
astonishment and admiration, "Who would have
thought it!"

The grandmother, too, followed the verses with the greatest attention but she did not say anything.

The following day at school when it was Peter's turn to read, the teacher said, "Well, Peter, must we pass you again or would you like to try?"

Without hesitation, Peter read three lines. The teacher laid down his book and stared at Peter as if he had never see him before. Then he said, "Peter, this is a miracle! With all the patience in the world I did not succeed in teaching you even your letters and here you are reading beautifully. How did this come about?"

"It was Heidi," Peter answered.

In surprise the teacher turned towards Heidi who sat on her bench looking as though nothing out of the ordinary had happened.

The teacher continued, "I have noticed a change in you altogether. You have been attending school very regularly lately. What can have brought about this change for the better?"

"The uncle," came the reply.

With ever-growing astonishment the teacher looked at Heidi, then back again at Peter.

As soon as school was over, the teacher hastened

to tell the pastor what had happened and what a good influence the uncle and Heidi had been.

Every night now Peter read a hymn in obedience to Heidi's instructions, but he refused to read a second one and indeed the grandmother never encouraged him to do so.

Brigitta was always delighted that her Peter had achieved so much but the grandmother said, "Yes, it is good that he has learnt so well but still I shall be glad when it is spring and Heidi can come up again. When Peter reads there always seem to be some words missing in the hymn so that I don't understand them so well as when Heidi reads them."

The reason was, of course, that Peter was rather lazy about reading for the grandmother and if a word was too difficult or too long, he just skipped over it thinking it would not matter very much to the grandmother, seeing there were so many words! Thus it was that most of the important words in the hymns were missing altogether when Peter read them.

CHAPTER 20

News From Clara

May had come again and from the heights the streamlets rippled eagerly down into the valley. The last snow had melted and the golden sun had dried up the last traces of winter. The spring breeze was rustling the tops of the old fir trees and last year's dark green pine needles were being replaced by bright, shiny light green ones. The great eagle flew high above, lazily circling in the blue air, and the warmth of the sunshine seeped into the ground beneath, and warmed the ancient timbers of the grandfather's hut. Heidi was happy to be on the Alm again and jumped about for joy, and it seemed to her that the little wild creatures which started about were as happy as she and all were humming and singing, "On the Alm!

On the Alm!" At one moment she would stand
listening to the strange sounds of the wind blowing
down from the mountain tops and bending the fir
trees until they strained with its force. Then she
would rush round to the front of the hut, and
sitting on the ground in the sunshine she would
watch the tiny flowers gradually opening in the
warmth of the sun. Joyfully, she followed the antics
of all the thousands of little insects going about
their lives in the glorious spring weather, All the,
while, she could not stop thinking how beautiful
the mountain looked.

Familiar sounds came from the carpenter's shed.
Heidi knew what the sounds meant, for they had
been familiar to her ever since her first arrival on the
Alm. The grandfather was busy finishing a beautiful
new chair and another one, already finished, stood
outside.

"Oh, I know what these are for!" cried Heidi.
"We will need them when they come from
Frankfurt. This one is for Grandmamma and the
one you are making now is for Clara. Will there be
another one, Grandfather?" she asked hesitantly.
"Perhaps Fräulein Rottenmeier is coming too."

"Well, I am not sure at the moment," replied the

grandfather, "but it is best to make an extra one just in case she does come."

Heidi gazed at the simple wooden chair, and couldn't imagine Fräulein Rottenmeier actually sitting down on it. After a few moments' contemplation she said doubtfully, "Grandfather, I really don't think that Fräulein Rottenmeier would be suitable for that chair."

"In that case she can enjoy the comfortable bed with the mattress of green grass," was the grandfather's reply.

Suddenly there was a great whistling and shouting and Heidi knew immediately it was Peter. She rushed outside and immediately found herself crowded on all sides by her animal friends. They too were delighted to be on the mountain once more, for they were frolicking and bleating with joy, nudging and pushing Heidi in their anxiety to show her how pleased they were to see her. A harsh command from Peter sent them scattering, however, for he had something to deliver to Heidi. There he stood brandishing a letter. It was addressed to Heidi.

"How did you get this?" she asked in surprise.

"I found it inside my dinner bag," replied Peter.

This was only partly true. The letter had been handed to him the previous evening by the postman at Dörfli, and Peter had put it at the bottom of his bag. This fine morning he had filled the bag with his bread and cheese and had completely forgotten about the letter when he collected the grandfather's two goats. He only remembered it when he had finished his lunch and was checking for any additional food which might have been missed. Carefully Heidi read the address, then ran towards the grandfather, holding out her letter. "From Frankfurt! From Clara! Do you want to hear it?"

Of course, both he and Peter wanted to hear it, so Heidi began to read:

"DEAR HEIDI,

Everything is packed and ready and in two or three days we shall be on our way. Papa will not be coming with us as he has to go to Paris first. The doctor comes to see me every day and as he comes into the room he always calls, 'Off you go now! Off to the Alm as quickly as you can!' He says everybody must become healthy and happy there. He, too, is his own self again after being with you. He

has come almost every day during the winter, and
has spent long hours telling me everything about
life up there. He tells me of all he did with you two,
and talks of the flowers and the light and the peace-
fulness of the mountains, high above the noise of
the towns and villages. And he takes a deep breath,
as though he were breathing your pure mountain
air, and says that no-one can fail to get better up
there. He is altogether changed since he saw you,
and looks much younger and happier. Oh, how I
am looking forward to seeing everything, to being
with you and also to getting to know Peter and the
goats! I have to go to Ragatz first, for six weeks, as
the doctor has ordered. Then we will go to Dörfli,
and every day, if the weather is good, I shall be
carried up to see you. Grandmamma is coming
with me and is looking forward greatly to seeing
you. But what about this: Fräulein Rottenmeier
has adamantly refused to join us. Grandmamma
often asks her if she would not like to accompany
us, but she always refuses, very politely of course.
Apparently Sebastian gave her a fright by empha-
sising the dangers of the mountains and the
precipices, and she quite lost interest in the idea of
a journey. Tinette is just as frightened, so

Sebastian will come with us as far as Ragatz, and we will finish the journey alone. I can hardly bear to wait. Good-bye, Heidi! Grandmamma sends her love,

> Your affectionate friend,
> CLARA."

Peter was not at all thrilled with the news of the arrival of the guests from Frankfurt. It made him very cross indeed and he ran outside, waving his stick in the air so wildly that he frightened the goats, and they scrambled down the mountain ahead of him. Peter tore after them, brandishing his stick as though he would strike someone.

He was furious at the thought of the prospective visitors, who would again take Heidi's company away from him. Heidi was overflowing with happiness. As soon as possible she called at the grandmother's to tell her the good news. She knew the grandmother would be interested in all she had to tell, for Heidi had talked to her of all the people who were to arrive, and she had sympathised with the troubles which had beset her life at Frankfurt. Heidi called on her in the afternoon, while the sun was high in the sky, and she raced down the mountain, with the breeze blowing her along. The grandmother was sitting spinning once more in her usual corner. She was no longer confined to bed, but although she was so much better her face wore an expression of sadness. Peter had told her the news about the people who were coming from Frankfurt and the grandmother had her own ideas of what might come to pass. She could not help dreading that they might take Heidi away again. Heidi rushed in, and sitting on her little stool began a stream of excited chatter about the events which were about to happen.

As she was in the midst of telling the grandmother the great news, she had to stop suddenly and ask with concern, "What is the matter, Grandmother? Aren't you happy about all this?"

"Yes, yes, I am glad for you, Heidi," said the old woman, trying to put on a more cheerful expression. "Is it that you think Fräulein Rottenmeier may come after all?" asked Heidi nervously.

"No, Heidi, don't worry," said the old lady. "Hold my hand, and I'll know that you're here with me. Perhaps it would be a good thing if you went, although I doubt if I could bear the parting."

"Grandmother, nothing would give me pleasure

if you could not bear it," said Heidi, and her voice was so positive that the grandmother thought that perhaps even if the Frankfurt people did want to take Heidi, she might refuse to go. But, oh dear, that too would be all wrong. She was anxious to hide her fears and suggested, "I know something, Heidi, that would calm my thoughts. Read the hymn for me which begins: 'All things will work for good.'"

Heidi quickly found the hymn and read:—

> All things will work for good
> To those who trust in Me;
> I come with healing in my wings
> To save and set thee free.

When she had finished reading the grandmother said, "Yes, that is right! If one trusts in God one knows that whatever happens is for our good. Read it once more so that we won't forget." Heidi repeated the verse, reassuring herself as well as her grandmother.

Heidi returned home as evening descended, and rejoiced to see the stars glittering overhead. Eventually, entranced by the vast sparkling sky she said to herself, "I understand now why we should be happy and go bravely on our way; it is because God knows what is best for us, and what will bring us most happiness." The stars twinkled back at her all the way home, where she found her grandfather also star-gazing, overwhelmed by the beauty of the night sky.

The month of May had seldom before been so beautiful and sunny.

The sky was clear blue day after day and the grandfather exclaimed repeatedly, "This is indeed a good year. The sun will make the plants grow strong and nourishing. Take care, Peter, that your flock doesn't get out of hand from overfeeding!"

Peter's answer could be clearly read in his face.

"I can manage them!"

May had passed and June arrived, bringing hot, long days filled with the scent of the flowers carpeting the mountainside. The month was drawing to its close when one morning Heidi ran out of the hut. She had intended to visit the fir trees and then climb up to see if the rock roses were in bloom. Just as she turned the corner she gave a loud cry which brought the uncle hurrying to see what had happened.

"Grandfather! Grandfather!" the child called excitedly, "Come over here! Come and look!"

He came, and his eyes followed the direction of her outstretched arm. A strange procession could be seen coming up the mountain path. In front came two men carrying a sedan chair in which a young girl sat, wrapped in many shawls. A horse followed, mounted by a stately lady who looked about her with keen interest. Another man pushed an empty wheel-chair, for it was easier and safer to carry the invalid up the mountain in the sedan.

"Here they are! Here they are!" cried Heidi joyfully.

When the eagerly expected guests reached the Alm, Heidi sprang forward and the two children embraced each other lovingly. Grandmamma, too, was welcomed with the greatest affection. Then Grandmamma turned to the Alm-Uncle who came forward to bid them welcome. They all felt like old friends, as they had heard so much about each other.

Grandmamma was delighted with the beautiful situation. "What a marvellous place to live, Uncle. I would never have believed it could be so very beautiful. You would be envied by the richest of

men. And how well my little Heidi is looking!" she remarked, patting the child's rosy cheeks. "What do *you* think, Clara? Isn't it delightful here?"

Clara was entranced. Never in her life before had she seen or imagined anything so beautiful. "Oh, how lovely it is! How I wish I could always live here with Heidi, Grandmamma!"

Meantime the uncle had pushed the invalid chair nearer and now he suggested, "Wouldn't it be better to put the little daughter into her accustomed seat?" And without waiting for assistance he lifted Clara in his strong arms and very gently placed her in her own comfortable chair, putting some of the wraps over her knees and doing it all as expertly as if he had looked after invalids all his life. Grandmamma was greatly impressed by his care and attention.

"If I knew where you had come by your skill, I would pack every nurse I know off to learn to handle their patients as gently as you. How on earth do you know what should be done?"

Alm-Uncle smiled sadly and said, "I know from my own experience." He saw again a painful scene of many years before, of a crippled man lying helpless and unable to move. It was his captain, who had been mortally wounded during some fierce fighting in Sicily. The Uncle had carried him from the battlefield and nursed him until his death.

Thus it had seemed easy and natural to him to adopt the role of nurse once again. Clara could not find words to express her delight in everything around her. "Oh, Heidi," she said, "if only I could go about and see all the things you have described to me!"

With a great effort Heidi succeeded in wheeling the chair on to the grass so that Clara could see the magnificent old fir trees which had gazed down undisturbed for so many years on the valley below. The sky extended a clear blue for as far as the eye could see, and Clara was fascinated. She had never seen such trees before. The grandmamma had followed them and was equally amazed at the appearance of strength of the magnificent great firs, which had seen so much change beneath their spreading branches. Heidi wheeled Clara to the goat-house next, and opened the door so that Clara could see inside.

"If only I could wait till Peter comes with the goats!" Clara said regretfully. "How I should love to see Little Swan and Little Bear! If we must always leave as early as you say, Grandmamma, we shall never see them!"

"My dear child, let us enjoy the things we can and not think of those we may miss."

"Oh, how pretty the flowers are! If only I could get up and pick some!"

Heidi ran and gathered a big bunch. "But that is nothing, Clara," she said. "If you come with us up to the pasture you will see ever so many. There are flowers of every colour you can think of, and they smell so lovely. There are so many there is hardly room to move amongst them. They are as thick as a carpet and if you sit down amongst them you never want to get up again."

Heidi's eyes sparkled with longing to be able to show it all to her friend, and Clara's soft blue eyes reflected Heidi's enthusiasm.

"Oh, Grandmamma! Do you think I shall ever be allowed to go up as high as that?" she asked. "If only I could go with you, Heidi! I should like to climb all over the Alm."

"I shall push your chair," said Heidi stoutly, and to show how easy it was she made a rush at the chair which nearly sent it rolling down the slope. But the

grandfather was near at hand and stopped it in
time.

Grandfather had been busy preparing the meal
and he had brought the table and the chairs
outside beside the bench. Soon the meal was ready
and the whole company sat down merrily.
Grandmamma was delighted with this dining-
room under the blue sky where she could sit and
enjoy the magnificent view far down into the
valley. "Can I believe my eyes?" she exclaimed
when she saw Clara taking a second helping of
toasted cheese which she was eating with a great
appetite.

"Yes, Grandmamma. It tastes so good. Better
than the whole menu at Ragatz," Clara assured her.

"That's right. Eat all you can," encouraged the
uncle. "Our mountain air makes up for the defi-
ciency of the kitchen."

Grandmamma and the uncle chatted together as
though they had known each other for years. They
had much in common and the time passed quickly
in lively conversation. But suddenly Grandmamma
remembered, "We will have to go presently, Clara.
The sun will be going down soon and the men with
the chair will be here."

"Just let's stay another hour, Grandmamma," pleaded Clara. "We haven't seen inside the cottage yet and we must see Heidi's bed."

Grandmamma wanted to see inside the cottage, too, and the uncle invited them to go in. Clara's chair, however, was too broad to pass through the door, but without hesitation, the uncle lifted Clara out of the chair and carried her inside.

Grandmamma looked around with interest and was very much impressed by the tidiness and cosy atmosphere of the house. "Is your bed up there, Heidi" she asked and started to climb up to the loft. "Oh, what a lovely scent! This should be a healthy bedroom," she exclaimed.

Grandfather followed, carrying Clara, and Heidi came after. They all stood around Heidi's bed. "Heidi, how jolly!" exclaimed Clara. "From your bed you can look straight up into the sky! And you will always have the lovely smell of the hay and will be able to listen to the fir trees rustling! It is quite the loveliest bedroom I have ever seen."

The uncle looked at Grandmamma. "I have an idea," he said. "I think if we could agree to have your little grand-daughter staying here with us for a while, she would be bound to get strong and well.

With all the rugs you have brought we could make
a fine soft bed and I myself would look after her."

Clara and Heidi were as happy as two birds let
out of their cage at this suggestion and the
Grandmamma's face beamed. "My dear Uncle,
you are kindness itself," she said. "I have just
been thinking how good a holiday so high up in
the mountains would be for the child. But the
nursing, the trouble and the inconvenience for
you! And you make the offer as if it were nothing
at all. I thank you from the bottom of my heart."
The old lady took his hand and the uncle nodded
happily. He carried Clara back to her chair
outside, with Heidi skipping along after them.
Then he picked up a huge pile of shawls and furs
which had been carried up the mountain for Clara
and said, "What a good thing Grandmamma
brought all these with her; they will be most
useful."

He at once started to get Clara's bed ready and
he and the Grandmamma spread the rugs over it.
When they had finished, the bed was so smooth and
thick, not a single bit of hay could penetrate.
Satisfied, Grandmamma climbed down the ladder
and joined the children who were already

discussing how they would spend their time. But, how long would Clara be allowed to stay, was the great question. Grandmamma replied, "Grand-father knows best. You must ask him."

The grandfather thought four weeks would be just right to decide if the mountain air was agreeing with the child. The prospect of being together for so long surpassed the children's expectations and they both shouted for joy.

The chair-bearers appeared at the cottage but they were immediately sent down the mountain again.

"It is not farewell, Grandmamma," said Clara as they parted. "You will come and visit us here on the Alm and see what we are doing and how we are getting on, won't you?"

Heidi could only express her happiness with a high jump.

Grandmamma mounted her horse and the Alm-Uncle set off to lead her down the mountain path. She tried to persuade him to go back, but he insisted on seeing her safely to Dörfli for it was a rocky and dangerous path for those who did not know it well.

She decided to return to Ragatz rather than stay

alone in Dörfli. From there she could equally well pay occasional visits to the Alm.

Peter and the goats arrived while the Uncle was escorting Grandmamma, and as soon as they saw Heidi the animals rushed towards her. She and Clara were soon in the midst of a pushing, nudging, bleating crowd. Clara made acquaintance with each and every one as Heidi introduced them, including little Snowflake, and Goldfinch, about whom she had heard so much.

Peter, meanwhile, stood sullenly to one side, not looking at all pleased at the attention being given Clara.

The two girls greeted him in a friendly way, but he turned on his heel, and waving his stick in the air, rushed off, with the goats following him.

The day closed for Clara with the most overwhelming experience of all. She lay in the big soft bed in the loft with Heidi near, and looked through the round open window right into the middle of the starlit sky. "Oh, Heidi!" she exclaimed. "It seems as if we were riding through the sky!"

"Do you know why the stars twinkle so happily?" asked Heidi.

"No, why do you think?"

"Because they see how well God has arranged everything for men so that nobody needs to be afraid and can be quite sure that everything will turn out for the best. But we must not forget to pray, Clara, and to ask God to remember us."

The children sat up and said their prayers together; then Heidi put her head on her arm and fell asleep at once. But Clara lay awake a long time. She had never been able to see the stars at home because she had never been outside the house at night, and inside, the heavy curtains were always drawn long before the stars came out. So she could not gaze long enough at the sparkling heavens and lay looking out of the little round window until at last her eyes closed of their own accord and she saw the stars in her dreams.

CHAPTER 21

Life on the Alm

The Alm-Uncle had been standing outside the hut as was his habit, watching the early mists rising and the new day awakening. The morning clouds grew brighter and brighter until the sun appeared in its full glory and flooded the rocks, woods and mountains with golden light.

The uncle went back into the hut and quietly climbed up the little ladder. Clara had just opened her eyes and did not know at first where she was. Then she saw the sleeping Heidi beside her and heard the kindly voice of the grandfather whispering, "Did you sleep well?"

Clara assured him that she had slept soundly all night. The grandfather was pleased and straight away began to attend to her so gently and sympathetically that one would think that he had been looking after sick children all his life. Now Heidi was awake and watched the grandfather carry Clara downstairs. Quickly she got up and dressed and ran down the ladder after them and out into the open air.

There a surprise awaited her, for the grandfather had not been idle after the children had retired for the night. He had noticed that it was impossible for Clara's chair to be carried through the hut door. So he loosened two boards at one side, which would allow for the chair to go through whenever required. Clara was just being wheeled into the sunshine. There he left her while he went to attend to the goats, and Heidi joined her friend.

The soft morning breeze touched their faces, and Clara could smell the fresh scent of the fir trees. She took a deep breath of pleasure and noticed how well and comfortable she felt.

She had never before been out in the country so early in the day, and it was sheer delight for her to breathe the clear mountain air and feel the warm sun caressing her face and hands. It was better than Clara had ever imagined it could be.

"Oh, Heidi, if only I could stay in the mountains with you always!" she exclaimed.

"Do you understand now why I said that the best place in the world is on the Alm with Grandfather?"

Just at that moment the grandfather appeared with two bowls of foaming milk. "This will give you strength," he said to Clara. "It is from Little Swan, and will help you regain your health."

Clara had never tasted goats' milk before and she smelt it first. But when she saw Heidi drinking hers to the last drop, she did the same. It tasted sweet and strong, as though it contained sugar and cinnamon. Soon her bowl was empty, too.

"To-morrow we may be able to take two," the grandfather suggested, observing with satisfaction how Clara had followed Heidi's example.

Soon Peter arrived with his flock and the uncle took him aside to tell him to be sure to take Little Swan high up where she would get the best grass. "She knows where the best food is, and if it should mean going a little higher, never mind. Follow her; a bit of extra climbing won't do you any harm. I want the best possible milk from her and you can ensure that she eats well. Why are you staring over there as though you wanted to eat somebody?" the grandfather exclaimed in the midst of his instructions. "Now be off! And remember what I have said!"

Peter marched off at once, but it was obvious that there was something going on in his mind. When Heidi appeared amongst the goats he said to her threateningly, "You had better come with me because Little Swan has to get special attention and someone will have to stay with the others."

"No, I can't," replied Heidi. "I can't come so long as Clara is with me. But Grandfather has promised that some time we shall come together."

As she said this she ran back to Clara and Peter made threatening gestures towards the invalid chair. Then he quickly climbed up until he was out of sight for he was afraid the uncle might have seen him.

Clara and Heidi had so many plans that they hardly knew what to do first. Heidi suggested that they should first write to Grandmamma for they had promised to write every day and tell her all their experiences.

"Must we write the letter inside the cottage?" asked Clara who preferred to stay outside and enjoy the lovely scenery.

Heidi went into the cottage to get all the things they needed and then they both settled down to write the letter. After almost every sentence Clara had to stop and look around. It was far too beautiful for writing. The wind was no longer cool, and gently caressed her face. Insects danced and hummed in the air and a deep silence lay on the sunny fields. The whole, broad valley lay peacefully below and only now and then was the silence broken by the yodelling of a shepherd boy, and the sound echoed softly amongst the rocks.

The morning passed so quickly, the children were surprised to see the uncle bringing the lunch which they took out of doors just as they had done the day before. He had decided that as long as there was a ray of light from the sun, the little daughter should have the benefit of the fresh air. In the afternoon they sat in the shadow of the fir trees and Clara related all the things that had happened at Frankfurt since Heidi left. The greater their animation as they talked, the louder chorused the birds above, as if they, too, wished to join in the conversation. Time flew past, and they hardly realised that the afternoon was nearly over.

Evening was approaching and the goats came rushing down the mountain, their keeper following them with a not very pleasant expression on his face. He did not even answer the children's friendly call but went on chasing the goats.

When Clara saw that the grandfather had taken Little Swan away for milking she suddenly felt very impatient to taste the milk. "Isn't it strange!" she said. "I never used to like to eat. Everything tasted like cod liver oil, and now I can hardly wait until supper-time when Grandfather brings the milk." Heidi understood—she remembered the dreadful times in Frankfurt, when she had felt unable to eat. Clara though, was puzzled. She did not realise that it was simply that she had never ever spent a complete day out-of-doors, let alone in the pure, healthy mountain air.

This time, when the milk arrived, Clara even finished hers before Heidi and asked the grandfather for a second helping. He nodded cheerfully, and taking both bowls, went back into the cottage. When he returned with the milk he brought two large slices of bread, spread with plenty of butter which he had got fresh from a herdsman's cottage that afternoon. It tasted delicious and the grandfather smiled with satisfaction to see the two children eat so heartily.

That night, when they went to bed, Clara wanted to look up again at the stars but her eyes would not stay open and she was soon fast asleep like Heidi and slept as she had never done before in her life.

So the days passed happily. One day the children were surprised to see two porters climbing up the mountain. Each of them carried a bed on his back, complete with sheets and mattress. The men also brought a letter from Grandmamma in which she said that the beds were for Clara and Heidi. She instructed Heidi to sleep in the proper bed, and to take it with her to Dörfli in winter, leaving the other behind, so that there would always be a bed for Clara if she visited. She also thanked the children for their letters and encouraged them to continue to write and tell her about everything that happened. The grandfather moved all the hay out of Heidi's room, and then enlisted help in moving the two beds up to the loft. There they were set close enough for both the children to be able to watch the stars.

Grandmamma was very pleased that Clara was enjoying the Alm so much and she was quite content to wait a little before she repeated her visit to the Alm because the ride up the steep mountain was rather trying for her.

Clara had now spent three weeks on the Alm and was enjoying life more every day. She could not praise sufficiently the love and care with which the grandfather nursed her. As for Heidi, her cheerful chatter and amusing companionship made her presence even more enjoyable than in Frankfurt. Every morning Clara expressed her delight in the good fortune which had brought her there.

Grandmamma decided, on the basis of the optimistic reports coming daily from the mountain, that she would postpone her visit for a while, for it was by no means an easy journey for her. During the last few days, when Grandfather carried Clara downstairs to put her into her chair he asked her, "Wouldn't the little daughter like to try to stand on the ground?" Clara had always tried to please him but had soon been forced to cry out, "Oh, it hurts!" and had clung to him; but each day he allowed her to stand just a little longer without her noticing.

For years they had not had such a splendid summer on the Alm. Every day the sun shone brilliantly out of a cloudless sky.

Heidi never tired of describing the high pasture to her friend. She talked of the golden light from the setting sun, and the myriads of beautiful flowers carpeting the ground. As she told Clara about the lovely rock roses and the vivid blue harebells she longed suddenly to be up there once again, and she sprang up and asked the grandfather, "Will you come to the pasture with us to-morrow?"

He consented. "But the little daughter must do me a favour too. To-night she must try her very best to stand."

Cheerfully Heidi ran with this news to Clara who promised to try to stand on her feet as much as ever Grandfather wanted, for she was looking forward immensely to this excursion.

As soon as Heidi caught sight of Peter in the evening she exclaimed, "Peter! Peter! To-morrow we shall come up too and stay all day on the pasture."

But Peter just grumbled like a bear in a temper and was about to give Goldfinch a hefty whack out of sheer bad feeling, but nimble Goldfinch saw what was coming and leaped out of the way in time.

That night Clara and Heidi went to their new beds full of anticipation of the next day. They agreed to stay awake all night to talk about their plans, but hardly had their heads touched the pillows when the conversation suddenly ceased. Clara saw in her dreams a big pasture thickly covered with flowers and Heidi heard the eagle crying, "Come! Come! Come!"

CHAPTER 22

An Unexpected Event

Early next morning the old man looked out to see what sort of day it would be. The dark shadows in the valley lifted and gradually a rosy light spread across the mountains until above and below were bathed in colour. The sun had risen. A gentle breeze was moving the branches of the fir trees back and forth as the sun caught the tips of the trees in its warm glow.

The uncle brought the invalid chair from the shed and placed it in front of the house, and then went inside to tell the children what a beautiful morning it was.

Peter came lumbering up the hill. All the jealousy and temper in him had reached a climax. For weeks he had not had Heidi to himself. Even the goats avoided him as much as they could, for he would brandish his stick and hit them hard without any justification, and they no longer trusted him as they had in former days. When he came in the morning the strange child was carried out to her chair and Heidi's attention was completely taken up with her. In the evening, the invalid was still there and again Heidi had no time for him. Not once, all during the summer, had Heidi come up to the pasture, and though she came to-day she would still be accompanied by her friend and would still have no time for him. Peter anticipated this and it made him quite wild with rage.

When he caught sight of the chair, standing so proudly on its wheels, it seemed to him that here was the enemy who had done all this harm to him and would, to-day, hurt him still more. There was no one about and everything was quiet. Wildly he rushed forward, and, seizing the chair, he pushed it with all his might down the slope. He pushed with such violence that it disappeared almost at once. Peter then rushed up the Alm and took cover behind a big black-berry bush. Here he was hidden from the uncle's sight but could watch the chair's progress down the mountain. Far below, he saw it gather speed, bouncing off the rocks until it turned

over and over and flew into a hundred pieces. The sight filled Peter with such an indescribable joy that he laughed aloud and stamped his feet. The boy raced round in circles, completely beside himself at the destruction of his enemy.

And now he thought of all the pleasant things for him which would result from the disaster. The stranger would have to leave because she could not get about without her chair; then Heidi would be free again to come with him up to the pasture. Everything would be as it had been in days gone by. It did not occur to Peter that if we do something wrong, trouble is sure to follow.

Presently Heidi came out and ran to the shed. The door was wide open. She looked everywhere, puzzled to know what had become of the chair.

"Did you move the chair, Heidi?" asked the grandfather.

"I have looked everywhere for it. You said it was by the door," replied Heidi.

The wind suddenly grew stronger and rattled the door of the shed, blowing it back against the wall with a bang.

"Grandfather, it must have been the wind,"

called Heidi. "Oh, if it has blown the chair down the valley we will never get it back in time."

"If it has rolled a far as that we will never get it back at all," said the grandfather. "By now it will be in a thousand pieces," and he went round the corner of the hut to look down the path. "It is very odd," he said to himself. "The chair would have had to have turned the corner outside the shed."

"Oh, what a pity! Now we can't go," lamented Clara "If I have no chair I am sure I shall have to go home. Oh, what a pity!" Heidi, however, looked confidently at her grandfather, and said, "You will help, won't you, Grandfather, so that Clara doesn't have to go home?"

"We will go to-day as we intended," replied the uncle. "Then we shall see what else can be done."

The children were delighted.

The uncle then went back into the hut and bringing out some of the rugs, spread them out on the sunniest spot for Clara to sit on. Then he brought the milk for the children and led Little Swan and Little Bear out of the shed.

"I wonder why the boy is not here yet?" thought the uncle, for Peter had not greeted them with his usual whistle that morning.

He picked up Clara and, carrying her on one arm and the rugs on the other he said, "Now, let's be off! The goats will come with us."

With one arm round Little Swan's neck and the other round Little Bear's, Heidi walked behind the grandfather. The little goats were so pleased to be with her again that they almost pushed her over with their loving nudges and squeezes.

When they arrived on the pasture they saw here and there on the slopes, goats peacefully grazing, and in the midst of them, on the ground, Peter was lying.

"I'll teach you to pass my house another time, you lazy fellow!" called the uncle "What does this mean?"

Peter shot up at the sound of the familiar voice. "There was nobody up," he answered.

"Did you see anything of the chair?" the uncle continued.

"Of what?" Peter answered back obstinately.

The uncle said no more but spread the rugs on the sunny slope and set Clara down upon them, asking if she was comfortable.

"As comfortable as in the chair," she said gratefully, "and I think this most be the most beautiful spot on earth. Oh, Heidi, how lovely it is!"

The grandfather got ready to leave them. "Enjoy yourselves!" he said. "When dinner-time comes, Heidi will get the food from the rucksack which I have put in the shade. Peter will provide the milk but Heidi must see that it is milk from Little Swan, and in the evening I will come back to fetch you. Now I must go and look for the chair and see what has happened to it." It was a truly beautiful day. The sky was a deep, clear, azure blue, and the high snowfields glittered as though covered in a thousand jewels. The great mountain summits rose majestically to the sky, and the great eagle hovered above. The wind blew down from the mountains and swept cool draughts of air around the children sitting in the sun.

The children had never been so happy together. The goats would gather round them in a friendly way and they had even got to know Clara well enough to rub their heads affectionately against her shoulder. Little Snowflake came to see Heidi most often, laying her head in Heidi's lap, and only going away when another goat pushed her out of the way.

So the hours went by, and Heidi thought she would like to go to her favourite spot where the flowers grew so profusely, and see if the cups were

open now and as beautiful as last year. Clara could
only be taken there in the evening when the grandfather came back, but by that time the flower bells
would have closed again. Heidi could not resist the
temptation to go and look. Hesitatingly she asked
Clara, "Do you mind, Clara, if I leave you for a few
minutes? I would so much like to go and see the
flowers. But wait!" Heidi had an idea She led
Snowflake up to Clara. "There, now! You won't be
lonely."

Clara encouraged Heidi to go. She was quite
content to be with the little goat. Heidi had thrown
some leaves into Clara's lap and Clara held them
out to Snowflake one by one. The little goat ate the
leaves slowly from her hands and seemed contented
and trusting in her new-found friend. As she sat
alone on the mountain and looked at the little
animal which seemed to look up to her for protection, she thought how wonderful it would be to be
able, one day, to help others instead of always being
dependent as she was now. A great many thoughts
came into her mind and she longed to be able to go
on living in the sun and to lead a useful life.

She suddenly felt extraordinarily happy, as if she
saw everything in a new and beautiful light, and in

a fit of gaiety she threw her arms round Snowflake's neck and cried, "Oh, Snowflake—it is so wonderful here; I would so like to stay here for ever with you."

Heidi reached the lovely flower patch and the ground seemed to be completely covered with sparkling gold. It was more beautiful than ever and she breathed in the sweet fragrance. Suddenly she turned and ran back to Clara, out of breath with excitement. "You must come and see it!" she called from a distance. "The flowers are so beautiful now and in the evening they may have changed. I can carry you, don't you think, Clara?"

Clara shook her head. "No, no, Heidi! You are much smaller than I. Oh, if only I could walk!"

Heidi looked about as if searching for something. Up above, Peter sat staring at the children, as if he couldn't believe his eyes. Didn't he destroy the hated chair so that the stranger would not be able to move about and here she sat beside Heidi? Heidi spotted Peter and called, "Come down, Peter!"

"No, I don't want to," was the reply.

"But you must! Come! I can't carry Clara by myself. You have to help me. Come quickly!" Heidi urged him.

"I don't want to," he shouted again.

Heidi came up the hill towards him. With flaming eyes she stood before him and said, "Peter, if
you don't come at once I shall do something which
you won't like at all, I can tell you!"

Fear seized Peter. He knew he had done something wicked which he did not want anybody to
know about and here was Heidi speaking as though
she knew all about it. What if she told the uncle!
Peter feared nobody so much as him. Tortured with
anxiety, he got up and went down to Heidi.

"I am coming, but you mustn't do what you
said," he pleaded timidly so that Heidi felt quite
sorry for him.

"There's nothing to be afraid of. Come with me
now."

Heidi told him to take Clara's arm and she would
support her from the other side. But the difficulty
was how to make her walk when she could not even
stand. So Heidi ordered Peter to give her his arm to
lean on and asked her to put her other arm firmly
round Heidi's neck. "Then we can carry you."

But Peter had never in his life before given his
arm to anybody and kept it stiffly by his body.

"That's not the way," said Heidi and showed him
how to do it.

But in spite of it all they did not get on very well. Clara was not light and the team was too unequal— down on the one side and up on the other. Clara tried to help by putting forward first one foot and then the other but she always drew them back quickly again.

"Put your foot down firmly," Heidi suggested.

"Do you think—" Clara hesitated.

But she obeyed, and ventured first one step on the ground and then another. The pain made her moan a little. Then she put a foot out again and cried joyfully that it was less painful already.

"Try again!" urged Heidi eagerly.

Clara went on trying, again and again, and suddenly she exclaimed, "I can do it, Heidi! Oh, I can! Look! I can make steps—one after the other!"

"Can you really walk now? Can you really walk all by yourself? Oh if only Grandfather were here!" cried Heidi. "You can walk, you can walk!"

Clara had still to hold on to both Peter and Heidi, but with every step she felt safer, and it was less and less uncomfortable.

Heidi was quite beside herself with joy. "Now we will be able to come here every day and you will be able to walk like me and you will be healthy! Oh,

this is the most marvellous thing that could have
happened."

Clara joyfully agreed. She could think of nothing
in the world more wonderful than being able to
walk around like normal people and never again to
have to lie all day in her invalid chair.

It was not far to the slope where the beautiful
flowers grew. The children could already see the
yellow and blue patches. Soon they reached it.

"Let's sit down here," said Clara. They sat down
in the midst of the flowers. Heidi thought she had
never seen it so beautiful before. Clara was silent,
overcome with happiness at the beauty around her
and at the wonderful prospect which had opened
up before her . . . the joy of being able to walk about
like other people. Surrounding her were the many
colours of the flowers waving in the grass, and their
mixed perfumes enveloped her in an aura of
fragrance, so that she could hardly believe the
beauty of it all.

Heidi thought of Clara's cure, and the thought
made everything so perfect that she wanted to shout
aloud with pleasure. Clara could not speak, she was
so totally overwhelmed by the prospect of new life
which had opened before her, and the perfection of

her situation. Peter was quiet, too, and lay quite still
on the ground. He was fast asleep. Occasionally,
Heidi ran to and fro to look more closely at the
groups of flowers, and whichever way she turned
they seemed to smell sweeter and to grow in greater
abundance.

The children remained there for a long time. It
was long past noon when some of the goats
approached the slope and started to bleat loudly.
They did not care to eat flowers, and they looked
like a small deputation with Goldfinch as their
spokesman, who had come to protest at the absence
of their companions. The chorus awoke Peter and
he remembered with a pang of misgiving his wicked
deed of the morning. He willingly obeyed Heidi's
every command in the hope that she would not
report him to the uncle. The three of them went
back to the pasture and had their meal, Heidi
running to get the bag, for unknown to Peter, her
threat to him had been related to Peter's dinner.
She had noticed the lovely things which her grandfather had packed for them, and had been pleased
at the thought of Peter sharing them, and she had
originally intended that he should pay for his mood-
iness by going without dinner. Since he had, after

all, complied with her wish to help Clara, she now divided the food equally into large helpings. They all three ate well, but although Peter ate up every bit as usual he did not enjoy it very much, tortured as he was by the fear of punishment.

Soon after they had finished, the grandfather appeared, climbing up the slope, and Heidi rushed towards him to tell him the good news. The grandfather's face brightened and he smiled happily at Clara. "You have made the effort and you have won," he said.

He lifted Clara up and with his left arm behind her she walked, with his strong support, much more confidently than before. Heidi skipped happily beside them. Then the grandfather lifted Clara into his arms. "We mustn't overdo it," he said. "In any case it is time to go home."

Later in the evening, when Peter arrived in Dörfli with his goats, a crowd of people had gathered. They were looking at something which lay on the ground. Peter wanted to see too, and eventually elbowed his way through. There lay the pitiful remains of Clara's chair. There was a part of the back and some red padding and a few shiny nails; it was clearly the same chair and although it was

broken beyond repair it was easy to see that it had
once been a beautiful piece of workmanship.

"I saw them carry it up," said the baker. "I bet it's
worth a lot of money. I wonder if somebody did this
deliberately? When the gentleman from Frankfurt
hears of this he is sure to investigate. Suspicion is
going to fall on all those who have been up on the
Alm lately. I'm glad I haven't been up there for two
years at least." "Alm-Uncle said that it may have
been the wind," said one of the women, admiring
the shiny red upholstery.

"Just as well," returned the baker, "for whoever
else might have been responsible for such a deed
would surely be in trouble if he were found."

Peter had heard enough. Stealthily he crept away
from the crowd and ran up the mountain path as
though the devil were after him.

He was in a terrible state by the time he reached
home. He would not answer when he was spoken
to, refused to eat, and went up to bed as soon as he
could, only to put his head under the sheets and
torture himself with fears about what was to happen
to him.

As the children lay in bed that night, looking out
at the stars, Heidi said, "I have been thinking all

day how good it is that God does not give us just
what we ask. He always knows of something better
for us."

"Why do you think that, Heidi?" asked Clara.

"Because when I was in Frankfurt I prayed to be
allowed to go home at once and when it did not
happen I thought God did not hear. But, you see, if
I had run away at once you would never have come
here and would never have got well."

Clara thought hard. "But, Heidi," she said, "that
would mean that we must never pray for anything
because God knows better than we do."

"Yes, Clara, but we must do it like this," Heidi
replied eagerly. "Every day we must thank God for
everything to let Him know that we haven't forgotten that it all comes from Him. But, you know, if we
don't get what we have asked for we must not think
that God has not heard, and stop praying. We must
say then, 'Now I know, dear Father, that you have
something better in mind and I am glad that you
will make it right in the end, no matter what
happens now.'"

"How well you can explain it, Heidi," remarked
Clara.

"Grandmamma explained it all to me and it

turned out to be true. But I think we have to thank
God particularly to-day because He has given us
this great happiness—that you can walk now."
They each silently prayed and thanked God from
the bottom of their hearts for His goodness to
Clara.

The following morning, the grandfather
suggested that they should invite the grandmamma
to the Alm because they had something new to
show her. But the children wanted to give
Grandmamma a great surprise and wanted to wait
until Clara could go for a little walk supported only
by Heidi. They thought it would be about a week
before this could happen and in their next letter
Grandmamma was eagerly invited to come for a
visit; but they did not give away the secret.

Every day walking became easier and less painful
for Clara and longer walks were undertaken. The
exercise gave her such an appetite that the grandfather had to cut the bread a little bit thicker every
day, and he was very pleased when he saw it disappearing.

So another week went by, and the day of the
grandmamma's visit approached.

CHAPTER 23

Promises to Meet Again

The Grandmamma wrote to announce the day of her arrival and Peter brought the letter up from Dörfli that morning. Everyone was already up and about and the goats were waiting for him in their customary high spirits. The grandfather stood looking with pleasure at his happy healthy brood. As Peter approached he slowed his pace, and handing the letter apprehensively to the Alm-Uncle he then turned quickly and fled back down the mountain.

"Grandfather," asked Heidi. "Why does Peter always behave now as if he expected to be punished for something? He is like the goats running away for fear of the stick."

"Maybe he, too, is afraid of the stick which he sometimes thoroughly deserves," replied the grandfather. Peter ran without stopping until he was out of sight. Then he stopped. He was nervous and jumpy, as if he expected someone to leap on him and arrest him at any moment.

Heidi tidied the hut in preparation for the grand-mamma's arrival, and when everything was in order the children sat down on the bench outside the cottage, ready to welcome her. The grandfather came and sat down beside them. He held in his hands a lovely bunch of gentians which he had picked that morning. Heidi ran forward every now and then to see if there was any sign of their guest's arrival. Soon she saw a group of people toiling up the mountain path. First there came a guide, and then a white horse on which rode the grand-mamma, and last of all a porter with grand-mamma's luggage. At last the procession arrived and the old lady caught sight of the children.

"Why, what is this?" she cried out. "Clara, you aren't in your chair! I can't believe my eyes!" And before even shaking hands with any one she still exclaimed, "Clara, is this really you? Your cheeks have become quite round and rosy. I hardly recog-nise you, child."

She came forward to embrace Clara, but Heidi quickly slipped from the bench, and, with Clara leaning on her shoulder, they walked slowly towards the grandmamma.

The old lady stood transfixed. Then she embraced her little grandchild, then Heidi, then Clara again. She gazed at them both speechlessly. At last she saw the Alm-Uncle who had been watching the proceedings with a broad smile. With Clara on her arm she walked with her to the bench, and, letting Clara sit down, she grasped the old man's hand.

"My dear Uncle! How can I thank you? This is your doing! Your care and nursing—"

"And God's sunshine and mountain air," interrupted the grandfather, smiling.

"And also Little Swan's good milk," put in Clara. "Grandmamma, you should have seen how much milk I have been drinking!"

"I can see it, Clara, by your cheeks! What a change! You have become plump and strong and taller, too. I simply can't take my eyes off You! But now we must send a telegram to my son in Paris. He must come at once—but I shan't tell him why. This will be the most wonderful surprise he has ever had. Uncle, have the men gone? How can we send a telegram?"

"They have gone, but, if you are in a hurry, I will call Peter. He will do it."

A piercing whistle summoned Peter and he came running down from the high rocks. His face was pale and drawn, for he was convinced that the moment of truth had arrived and that Uncle was about to hand him over to the police. He was given a piece of paper on which the message was written and the uncle told him to take it to the post office at Dörfli. Peter hurried away, quite relieved to see that no policeman had arrived so far.

So now, everyone sat down to a delicious meal outside the hut, and grandmamma was regaled with elated accounts from all sides of the progress made with Clara, and the way in which her cure had come about. They told her how grandfather had persuaded Clara to do a little every day, first standing, then taking a few steps, and how, finally, after the chair had blown down the mountain, they had managed to take Clara up to the pasture. Grandmamma could hardly believe all that had taken place, and exclaimed with delight at every turn of events.

Clara and Heidi were of course beside themselves at Grandmamma's reaction.

In Paris, Herr Sesemann had finished his business and he also had a surprise in store. Without giving any warning, he took the train to Basle, for he had a great longing to see his little daughter from whom he had been separated all summer. He arrived at Ragatz a few hours after his mother's departure, and this fitted in nicely with his plans. He took a coach to Mayenfeld, where he learned that he could drive as far as Dörfli. The climb from there seemed to him very long and fatiguing, and when the cottage failed to come into view he began to wonder uneasily if he had chosen the right path or if the hut was on the other side of the mountain. He looked around, but no human being was to be seen of whom he could ask the way. He was beginning to wonder uneasily if he was on the right track. Just then, a boy came running from above; it was Peter with the telegram. He did not keep to the footpath but ran straight down the mountainside. Herr Sesemann beckoned to him and reluctantly Peter came forward.

"Come here, boy!" Herr Sesemann encouraged him. "Tell me, is this the way to the hut where the old man lives with the child, Heidi, and where the people from Frankfurt are staying now?"

A gasp was the only answer that came from Peter, and in his haste to get away, the boy fell head over heels and catapulted down the mountainside, just as the chair had done—except that Peter did not break up into pieces! The telegram, however, was torn to scraps.

"What a timid boy!" exclaimed Herr Sesemann, thinking that the appearance of a stranger had had this extraordinary effect on the simple boy of the mountains. And he continued on his way.

Peter had been convinced that this was the policeman from Frankfurt. He was overcome with terror at the sight of the visitor and was utterly certain that he had been sent to collect him and take him away to Frankfurt. He tumbled on down the mountainside until at last he managed to catch hold of a bush. He had to lie still for a moment or two to recover, and then he picked himself up.

"Well, well, and what is this that comes hurtling down the mountain?" said a voice behind him. Peter jumped, and saw the baker standing there chuckling. He had been most amused to see Peter tumbling down the mountain just like the chair had done.

Peter did not answer but began to scramble back up the slope. He wanted to go home and hide, but the goats were still up there waiting for him, and he dared not delay for fear of fresh recriminations from the Uncle. He was in a sorry state: bruised and shaken from his fall, and in an agony of fear and apprehension about the fate that was to befall him.

Shortly after meeting Peter, Herr Sesemann reached the first hut and knew that he was on the right road. So he climbed higher and higher and at last, after a long, strenuous walk, his goal came in sight. There stood the Alm hut.

Herr Sesemann joyfully climbed the last steep path. Before he had reached the top he was recognised by the party outside the cottage and quickly a surprise was prepared for him. As he left the path to approach the hut, two figures came towards him. A tall girl with fair hair and rosy cheeks leaned on her smaller companion. Herr Sesemann stood still and stared at them.

"Papa don't you know me?" called Clara. "Have I changed so much?"

At once Herr Sesemann rushed to embrace his little daughter.

"Yes, you have changed indeed! Is it possible?

Can this be my little Clara?" he exclaimed repeatedly.

Grandmamma had come forward. "My dear son, what do you think of this?" she cried. "You had prepared a pleasant surprise for us but I think we have an even pleasanter one for you! But now you must meet the Alm-Uncle who is our greatest benefactor."

"Gladly, and also our dear little Heidi," replied Herr Sesemann, shaking hands with Heidi. "I don't need to ask if you are well and happy. No alpine rose could look more blooming."

Heidi looked up with sparkling eyes at the kind Herr Sesemann who had always been so good to her. How glad she was that he could find such happiness on the Alm.

Then the grandmamma led her son to the Alm-Uncle. As the two men shook hands, Herr Sesemann expressed his heartfelt thanks and his great astonishment at the miracle.

Her eyes filled with tears, and the grandmamma turned away and looked towards the ancient fir trees. A patch of blue caught her eye. It was a beautiful bouquet of blue gentians. "How exquisite!" she exclaimed. "Heidi, did you pick them for me?"

"No," replied Heidi, "but I think I know who did."

Suddenly, a slight rustling sound came from behind the trees. It was Peter. At the sight of the strange gentleman with the Alm-Uncle, he had tried to slip away unobserved. But the grandmamma recognised him. She thought that perhaps it was he who had brought her the flowers, and that he was sidling along in the background from shyness at the possibility of her discovering them. She felt that she should reward him for his kindness. "Come here, my boy," she said loudly. "Don't be afraid."

Paralysed with fright, Peter looked out from behind the trees. "It is all up now!" he thought. His face distorted with terror, he began to creep forward.

"Come along now," encouraged the grandmamma. "Now tell me, boy, did you do this?"

Peter never lifted his eyes and, of course, did not see where the grandmamma's finger pointed. All he had noticed was the uncle standing at the corner of the hut, looking piercingly at him, and, what was most terrifying of all, beside him stood the policeman from Frankfurt. Trembling all over, Peter could only mutter something which sounded like "Yes."

"Well, what is so dreadful about that?" asked the grandmamma.

"That it is broken to pieces and can't be put together again." With great difficulty Peter managed to stammer the words and his legs shook so much he could hardly stand.

Grandmamma went over to the Alm-Uncle. "My dear Uncle, is there something seriously wrong with the poor boy?" she asked sympathetically.

"Nothing," replied the uncle, "but I think the lad may have been the 'wind' which chased the invalid

chair down the mountain and now he is expecting
his well-deserved punishment."

Grandmamma could hardly believe this for she
did not think he looked such a bad boy; and there
seemed no reason for him to destroy the chair. But
to the uncle, Peter's confession only confirmed the
suspicion which he had had from the beginning.
The angry looks Peter had cast on Clara and the
signs of resentment towards the newcomers to the
Alm had not escaped the uncle. He had put two and
two together and explained it all now to grandmamma. When he had finished, the lady said, "No,
no, my dear Uncle, we don't want to punish the
poor boy any more. One must be fair. We strangers
have, for weeks, taken Heidi away from him, so he
sits, day after day, and broods all by himself. No,
no, we must be fair. Anger and resentment drove
the boy to his revenge which was, perhaps, a little
foolish; but we are all foolish when we are angry."

Grandmamma went over to Peter and sat down
on the bench under the fir trees. In a kind voice she
said, "Come, my boy, stand in front of me. I want
to speak to you. Stop trembling and listen. You
pushed the chair down the slope to destroy it; that
was wicked and you knew that you deserved to be

punished. So to avoid that you took a lot of trouble
to hide the truth; but you see, he who does something wrong and thinks nobody will find out is
always mistaken. God sees and hears everything
and when He notices that somebody wants to hide
a wrong deed He wakes up the little watchman
whom He has placed inside us from our birth and
who sleeps inside us until we do something wrong.
This little watchman has a little prong in his hand
and he prods us with it all the time so that we do not
have a minute's peace. His voice torments us, too,
for it keeps calling. 'Soon you will be found out!
Now they'll come and drag you away!' So we live in
terror and anxiety and never have a moment's
happiness. Did you feel something like that, Peter?"

Peter nodded penitently, for that was exactly how
he had felt.

"In still another way you miscalculated, for you
wanted to do something wrong and something
good came out of it. Because Clara had no chair
and she wanted to see the beautiful flowers she tried
hard to walk; and she succeeded, and in the end,
was able to go every day to the pasture—much
more frequently than she would have done in the
chair. You see, Peter, God can turn evil into good

for the one who was meant to be harmed; harm comes to the evil-doer instead. Do you understand, Peter? If so, don't forget; and if you ever again want to do something wrong, remember the little watchman inside with his prong and unpleasant voice, will you?"

"Yes, I will," answered Peter, very depressed for he still did not know how the affair would end.

"Then everything is all right and the whole matter is settled," finished the grandmamma. "But now you shall have a souvenir from the Frankfurt visitors. Tell me, my boy, what would you like?"

Slowly Peter lifted his head and gazed at the grandmamma in astonishment.

He had expected some awful punishment and now he was being asked what he would like. He was completely confused.

"Yes, I am quite serious," continued the grandmamma "You shall have something as a remembrance and as a token that the people from Frankfurt think no more than that you did something wrong. Do you understand, my boy?"

Now it began to dawn on Peter that he need not fear any punishment and that the kind lady had saved him from arrest by the police. It was a great

weight off his mind. Now he saw, too, that it was
better to confess at once if one had done something
wrong and suddenly he stammered, "And I also lost
the paper."

The grandmamma had to think for a moment
what this meant but soon she recalled the telegram
and said kindly:

"That is right. Always confess at once what you
have done and everything will be all right. And now
have you any special wish?"

Peter felt quite giddy at the thought of being able
to have anything he wanted. The annual fair at
Maienfeld flashed before his eyes with all the beautiful things he had admired so often and never
hoped to possess. There were the red whistles,
which he could use for his goats; and the fascinating
knives. Peter was deeply absorbed in his thoughts
and he could not decide which of the two he would
like the better. Suddenly he had a brainwave. "A
penny," he said.

The grandmamma laughed. "That is not an
extravagant wish," she said. "Come here!" She
pulled out her purse and took from it four bright
round shillings and on top of them she put four
pennies. "Well, we want to settle our accounts,"

she said. "I will explain it to you. Here are just as many pennies as there are weeks in the year and so you will be able to spend a penny every week for a whole year."

"All my life?" asked Peter innocently.

Now the grandmamma could not help laughing heartily so that the gentlemen interrupted their talk to hear what was going on.

"Yes, my boy, that's a passage for my will," said the old lady. "I will put down, 'A penny a week to Peter as long as he lives.'" Herr Sesemann nodded his agreement and laughed too.

Peter looked once more at the present in his hand. He still could hardly believe his eyes. Then he said, "God bless you!" and off he went, running and leaping, all fear and anxiety gone. His joy sent him flying over the rocks and boulders with twice his usual agility. He was forgiven, and he was to have a penny every week for the rest of his life.

After dinner, Clara took her father aside and said to him, "If you only knew, Papa, what the grandfather has done for me! I shall never forget it all my life. And I keep wondering, what could I give him or do for him, that would give him half the pleasure he has given me!"

"That is my dearest wish, too, my child," replied her father.

Herr Sesemann now went to the Alm-Uncle and seizing his hand, said, "My dear friend, let us have a word together. Believe me when I say that for years I have not known such happiness. Money and possessions have meant nothing to me since they have not helped to make my poor child well and happy. You have restored her health and given new life to her and me. Now, tell me, how can I show my gratitude? I can never repay what you have done, but whatever is in my power is at your disposal. Tell me, my friend, what can I do?"

The Alm-Uncle had listened in silence. Now he looked at Herr Sesemann and smiled. "Believe me, Herr Sesemann, I too am over-joyed at the girl's recovery on our Alm and my trouble has been well repaid by that. For your kind offer I thank you, but there is nothing I need; as long as I live I have enough for Heidi and myself. But if one wish only could be fulfilled I should have no more worries in this life."

"Speak, my dear friend," urged Herr Sesemann.

"I am old," continued the uncle, "and cannot expect to be here much longer. When I have passed away there will be nothing for the child and she has no relatives of any account. If you will promise that Heidi will never have to go out and earn her living among strangers then you will have amply repaid what I have done for your child."

"But there could never be any question about it!" exclaimed Herr Sesemann. "The child is one of us. Ask my mother and my daughter. They will never allow Heidi to go to strangers. This I promise you, both during my life and after, the child will never have to go among strangers. But she has made good friends, one of whom is our friend, the doctor. He is winding up his affairs and intends to come and settle here this autumn, in the Swiss mountains, for he has never felt so well and happy as in the company of you and the child. You see, Heidi will now have two protectors. May they both live long!"

"God grant that will be so!" added the grandmamma and shook hands warmly with the Alm-Uncle. Then she embraced Heidi, who stood beside her.

"And you, my dear Heidi, come, tell me, don't you have a particular wish?"

"Yes, certainly," replied Heidi, looking cheerfully up at the grandmamma.

"What is it child?" she encouraged.

"I would like my bed from Frankfurt with the three high pillows and the thick cover, so that Grandmother needn't lie with her head downhill and won't need to put her shawl on in bed any more because she is cold."

"My dear child, it is good you remind me to think of others in our happiness, those who are not so well off as we are. I will wire at once to Frankfurt. The bed will be here in two days and, with God's help, the grandmother will soon be sleeping comfortably in it."

Heidi skipped delightedly round the grand-mamma. She wanted to go down at once and give the grandmother this happy message for she felt she had been away from her far too long, especially since the grandmother was in such discomfort the last time Heidi had seen her, but the grandfather said reprovingly, "No, no, Heidi! When you have guests you can't run away like that!"

But the grandmamma supported Heidi. "My dear Uncle, we shall go together. We can then go on to Dörfli and send the wire off to Frankfurt. What do you think, my son?"

Until now Herr Sesemann had not given much

thought to his holiday plans. Originally, he had thought of taking a trip through Switzerland with his mother and had wondered if Clara would be fit to accompany them for part of the journey. But now he would be able to enjoy the company of his daughter more fully. He did not want to miss any of these beautiful days of late summer and decided to stay the night at Dörfli and the next morning to fetch Clara when all three would go to Ragatz and start their journey from there.

Clara was a little upset at the thought of leaving the Alm but there was so much to look forward to and so little time to think that he was soon quite cheerful again. Heidi bounced for joy as they all went down the mountain. She told grandmamma all about the grandmother, and how cold she was, and what she lacked in the way of food.

Brigitta was standing outside the cottage when the little company approached and she rushed inside quickly crying, "They are coming, Mother."

"Alas, it is true, then," sighed the grandmother. "Do you think they are taking the child with them? Did you see her?"

Presently the door flew open and Heidi rushed into the room, going at once to the Grandmother's corner and embracing her affectionately.

"Grandmother, Grandmother! My bed is coming from Frankfurt, and the three pillows and also the thick cover. It will be here in two days. Grandmamma has promised."

The grandmother smiled a little sadly, "What a kind lady! I wish I could be happy that she is taking you with her, Heidi."

"What is all this? Who has been telling my good, old grandmother such tales?" said a kind voice. Grandmamma had overheard the conversation.

"No, no, that is out of the question! Heidi will stay with the grandmother, but we will come back to the Alm every year for we have good reason to thank God for this spot, and especially for the miracle He has wrought on our girl."

The grandmother's face lit up. Unable to speak, she pressed Frau Sesemann's hand again and again, and two large tears ran down her wrinkled cheeks.

Heidi clung affectionately to her and said, "Hasn't it all happened as in the hymn I read to you? When the bed comes from Frankfurt you will be much better too, Grandmother."

"Ah, yes, Heidi. God has sent me so many good things. Is it possible that there are such kind people who trouble themselves about a poor old woman?"

"My good Grandmother," interrupted Frau Sesemann, "in the eyes of God we are all equally poor and need His help; and He does not forget us. We must say good-bye now, but only until we meet again next year, and we certainly never will forget the dear grandmother."

Frau Sesemann took the grandmother's hand again, and with the old woman's blessing, Herr Sesemann and his mother continued their journey down into the valley.

Next morning, Clara was very sad about leaving the Alm where she had been so happy; but Heidi did her best to comfort her. "Summer will soon come again, and then it will be better still, for you are well now and we can go every day with the goats up to the pastures."

Clara dried her tears, "Don't forget to remember me to Peter and the goats," she said. Heidi suggested that Clara send Little Swan some salt, for she loved to lick some from out of the grandfather's hand in the evening. Clara promised to send a hundred pounds of salt so that Little Swan would never forget her.

Herr Sesemann had arrived and was beckoning to the children for it was time to go. Heidi stood at the very edge of the slope and waved to Clara until she disappeared from sight.

Frau Sesemann did not forget how cold it could be in winter on the mountain. She sent a big parcel to Goat Peter's hut; it contained warm clothing of every description so that the grandmother would never again have to sit trembling with cold.

The doctor arrived in Dörfli, and, on the Alm-Uncle's advice, he bought the house where the old man and Heidi stayed during the winter. The doctor decided to have it rebuilt, part of it for himself and the other part for the uncle and Heidi for their winter lodgings.

As the days went by, the doctor and the Alm-Uncle became very good friends and often their conversation would turn to Heidi because, for both of them, it was the greatest joy to have the child with them in their new house.

One day, when the doctor and the uncle were standing together, seeing how the new building was getting on, the doctor said to the old man; "I share your happiness in the child and I feel I am the nearest to her after you; I want to share also the responsibilities and to provide for her as best I can, so that I may hope that in my old age she will stay with me. That is my greatest wish, that Heidi should have the same claims on me as though she were my own child. Then we will be able to leave her free of worries when you and I have departed."

The grandfather pressed the doctor's hand and the doctor could read in the eyes of his friend how greatly touched he was by these words.

At this moment Heidi and Peter were sitting with the grandmother. Heidi had such a story to tell them that she hardly took time to breathe. They had seen very little of each other during the summer, and how much had happened!

It was difficult to tell which of the three radiant faces shone most happily.

Brigitta, with Heidi's help, at last understood the story of Peter's miraculous weekly penny and her face beamed, perhaps most radiantly of all.

At last, the grandmother said to Heidi, "Read one of the hymns to me, child! I want to thank our Heavenly Father for all the mercy He has bestowed on us!"